# Galin

## MYSTIC PROTECTORS SERIES   BOOK 3

## KATHI S. BARTON

This is a work of fiction. Names, characters, places, and incidents are products of the author's imagination or are used fictitiously and are not to be construed as real. Any resemblance to actual events, locations, organizations, or person, living or dead, is entirely coincidental.

# WCP

**World Castle Publishing, LLC**
Pensacola, Florida

Copyright © Kathi S. Barton 2014
Print ISBN: 9781629891705
eBook ISBN: 9781629891712
First Edition World Castle Publishing, LLC, October 27, 2014
http://www.worldcastlepublishing.com

**Licensing Notes**

Cover: Karen Fuller
Editor: Maxine Bringenberg

# Dedication

To my very own Denise Bush. You keep me straight, sane…well, sort of sane and you make me shine. I could not, nor would I want to do this without you. Simply put, you are the best at whatever you do. Thank you from the bottom of my heart and then some for everything!!! You rock it girl!!!

# Prologue

Michael moved down the hall toward the office. He knew that the other protectors hated to be summoned to this particular office, but he didn't mind. He loved going in and conversing with the Creator of all things. Boss, as He wanted everyone to call Him—as it sounded so much friendlier—was a man of men. A kind yet firm man, and one who could change things in a hummingbird's heartbeat. Michael paused in mid-step.

He was going to change things again. Things were running very smoothly right now, and He'd want to shake things up a bit. Michael tried to think what it could possibly be, and looked up when someone laughed.

"I was thinking." Boss nodded. "Am I going to regret coming here today?"

"Possibly. And I know you were thinking. I heard. You think much too hard for a man who has it all." Michael snorted, a habit he'd been trying to break himself of. "You think I would lie to you?"

"Nay. I think you believe whatever you wish will be wonderfully simple when it seldom is." Boss moved back into the room He'd come from, and Michael followed. The walls were covered with images of the protectors.

Protectors had long since been the ones who helped Boss in His daily work. A chosen man or woman would be given the assignment to watch over a child when they took their first breath. They never interfered with the person but whispered advice, gave them guidance, and when the time was right, they would be there with them when they drew in their last breath.

"I do wish to change things. But not for all of my protectors—just a few." Michael sat down, knowing that he'd have to carry out these duties no matter what they were. "You have noticed that they are...unhappy?"

"I have. But it's happened before. They are bored. The last time this happened we gave them a few days to interact on earth and they were happier for it." Boss shook His head. "You do not want that again."

"They wish to leave me." Michael sat there, stunned. He'd not heard that. But he knew to leave here would mean.... "I don't want that to happen."

"No, nor do I. Who is it? Maybe I can talk to them." Boss shook His head again. "You don't mean to kill them, do you? I know that is the way of things. When a servant is ready to end their time as a protector, they are sentenced to.... Please tell me of your plan." He was worried, as worried as he'd ever been when this happened. As much as they loved the job, there was only so much they could take. Michael missed them terribly.

"I wish to have them...perhaps it would be best if I showed you what I have in mind." The wall took another shape and images, a great many of them, started to move. The faster they moved, the more movie-like they became. Twice Michael had to ask him to slow down, and after He explained it to him, it moved on. Michael sat there for a long while after the movie stopped, and stared at the images of the few men he'd seen there. They were men of worth, men he would never have thought of being unhappy in what they did.

"They will not be happy with your interference. I believe they will be most upset with you." Michael looked at Boss when He didn't say anything. "Nor will Tholan. He will believe that he is not worthy of such a gift. He does not think himself worthy of much of anything."

"He will be the hardest to convince, yes, but if we deal with him later, then perhaps he will see it is not such a bad thing to have happen to him." Michael doubted that. Tholan had a weight on his heart that no one seemed able to help him with. "I would like to start with these five men before Tholan. I want...do you think you could help me get this started?"

"When would you like for this to happen?" Michael was looking over the files when he realized he'd not been answered. "You have already started this, haven't you?"

"I thought it best that we do some arranging to make sure that the other half of my project was well within hand for us." Boss laughed. "Do not look so crestfallen, Michael. The new group, my Mystics, will be a greater force than we ever imagined. You will see. They will be the best we have turned out in forever."

They worked well into the night, and when Michael left His office, Boss was smiling. Michael would be, too, if he wasn't so worried about Tholan. The man...well, that would be something they'd deal with at a later time. But now he had to give the list of men to him and hope that he didn't ask too many questions.

"It is going to be a long time before we will be able to say this worked." Michael heard Boss laugh and flushed. "You should come with me. He will have a fit."

"Nay, he will not. He is a good man. But a man who feels he has failed many. You'll do fine." Boss laughed again. "You are the Archangel Michael, men tremble at the sound of your name."

Eighteen months later

Dusty McGee watched the second hand move around the clock face. It would only need to pass the twelve eighteen more times before she could go in and see her sister again...if Rose lived that long. It had been a long and hard week, and she had a feeling it wasn't going to get much better. She looked over at Kip, her sister's son, as he sat beside her. He was watching the clock too.

"You can go first." He glared at her and she took a deep breath. "They will only let us stay there for ten minutes, and I thought you'd want to go in first this time. She might be—"

"I don't care if I ever see her again. What the hell was she thinking, anyway?" Dusty didn't answer him, because frankly she had no idea what her sister had been thinking. Not on the day she'd been hurt, nor when she'd decided what the lawyer had told Dusty about just that morning. But Kip didn't know that part yet. Dusty was still trying to deal with what she'd been told.

"You don't mean that. Not seeing your mom again will hurt you someday." He got up and she was again surprised at how tall he'd gotten. "Kip, she's your mom, no matter what she's been doing."

"Fuck off." His favorite thing to say to her since she'd arrived last week. And when he walked away from her, she didn't go after him this time. To be honest, he was wearing her out more than visiting her dying sister was.

Eight days ago she'd been on her way to work when she'd gotten a phone call. A very nice officer had told her that her sister had been in an accident and was asking for Dusty. This had happened before with Rose. She'd get in a jam, hurt herself, and call for Dusty to bail her out. Dusty was ready to tell the officer she didn't have time when he cleared his throat. In that second she knew this time was different.

"She's not going to live long, Miss McGee. The car that hit her knocked her into a busy intersection and she was hit three more times before she was thrown from the car. Her injuries are...they're horrific, and her body is broken."

"Where is Kip? Her son? Was he with her?" He didn't say anything for several seconds and she knew he was thinking of a way to tell her he'd not made it. "Please tell me he went quickly."

"We weren't aware there was a boy. I'm sending someone to her house now. Do you know anything that would help us talk to him?" Did she? Not really. She barely knew the boy herself since she and Rose had parted company about eight years ago.

"He's twelve now...no wait, not yet. He's eleven. But he has a mouth on him like an adult and will cut you to ribbons without a single thought." She closed her mouth when she realized what she'd just said. "I'm sorry. I'm...I'm on my way. I'll be there in the...where will I be coming to?"

"Mercy General. She's in surgery now but I had to assure her I'd call you before she'd let them take her in." Sounded like Rose, stubborn to a fault. "Do you need someone to pick you up?"

"Actually, I need more than that. I don't know where my sister has been for the past eight years. We never were very close." She pulled off the highway and sat there wiping at the tears. "Is she really dying? I mean, she's pulled crap like this before. Having someone call me to tell me she was grave, only to find her healthy as an ox when I got there. Tell me this is like that. I won't be mad, I swear I won't. I'll just give her whatever it is she wants and leave again. It's become a game we play. I don't particularly like it but she seems to get a laugh out of it. And some of my money."

"I'm sorry, Miss McGee. This is the real deal." He told her what city and state her sister was in and asked her if she wanted him to pick her up at the airport. She told him no, that she'd rent a car. When she hung up, Dusty called her assistant.

"I'm going away for a few days. There's some family problems I have to take care of." Denise Bush laughed. "I'm serious. My sister has had an accident."

Denise's tone changed in an instant. "How bad? And don't worry about a thing. I'll take care of it. Will you need for me to set some things up for you? Hotel, car rental while there?" Dusty loved this woman because of all she was. "I'm calling in a few favors now to get you whatever you need. Wait, it might help if I knew where you needed this done. And how soon you have to be there. You aren't there yet, are you? That would be so like you to simply go without telling me what was going on."

"Denise?" She shut up, and after Dusty explained where she was going she hung up. It wasn't until she was at the airport that she realized she might not make it to see Rose. That had been so long ago, and now Dusty wasn't sure she'd ever feel as if she wasn't in a dream. A nightmare, she supposed.

"Miss McGee?" She looked up at the man who was smiling down at her, bringing her from her daydreams. "It's time for you to see her again. I've looked for Kip but he said that he…there he is coming now."

Dusty followed the man, a male nurse, down the hall again. She had no idea why it was so far away from the intensive care unit, but it seemed miles since she'd gotten up. When they were outside the door he turned to look at her.

"I was told you wanted us to be honest with you from the start. And I will be now. She will not be with us much longer. If you can, I would suggest you say your goodbyes now."

Dusty nodded and looked down the hall as Kip came toward her.

"I will allow you both in together this time. Please, stay as long as you wish. As I said, it won't be long now."

Kip took her hand and she squeezed it tightly. As they entered the room the machines keeping her sister alive were eerily quiet. She looked at the form on the bed, having just yesterday stopped thinking of the broken body as just that and trying instead to think of her as her sister, a broken woman who would die soon. When the officer had told her Rose was bad, he'd not even been close to what had happened to her.

"Mom?" Kip moved to the bed and held his mother's hand. Dusty stayed back, giving him all the time he needed. She tried to think of the last time she'd spoken to her sister and all she could remember, like every time she tried to remember, was that they'd fought…as they did all the time. When Kip looked at her she realized that he had said something.

"She's going to die, isn't she?" Dusty nodded and moved toward him. "What the heck am I going to do now? I have nothing. They won't let me...I called a lawyer, and he said that I wouldn't be able to stay in my house any longer, that I wasn't old enough. Not to mention, it's not even ours. I'm all alone and I don't have a fucking clue what to do."

"You're coming with me. She—your mom—made arrangements for me to take care of you if anything should—"

"I'm not going with you. I don't even like you. And neither does my mom. Why the hell would she say something like that?" He looked down at the one person who had made them related. "You're a liar just like she said you were. I'm not going anywhere with you. Mom will get better, you'll see. And then I'll make sure that she never needs you again. I'll take care of her, you'll see."

Her heart, already so tender she wasn't sure if it was beating or not, shattered. He started sobbing and she wanted to go to him, even took a step toward him, when the machine near Rose's head started screaming at them. She was shoved out of the way as two nurses came into the room, but neither of them made a move toward her sister. It had been predetermined by Rose that if she was too far gone for them to try to resuscitate, they would let her die peacefully...or in this case as peacefully as she could. They all watched as the machines finally stopped. The monitor over her head simply straight lined. Dusty knew then that her sister was truly gone.

Dusty stepped into the hall when the doctor pronounced her gone and tried to think what she should be doing now. Nothing came to mind. She could hear Kip in the room screaming at them to wake her up, but Dusty had to get away. She was moving to the front doors when a man stepped in front of her.

"You will survive this." She shook her head and tried to step around him, but he moved with her. "Look at me, Dusty. You will survive this. And you will be stronger for it. Kip will learn to love you. He'll come to need you more than—"

"Stronger? I've never been strong in my life. My sister is dead and her son hates me. And as of twenty seconds ago, he's my responsibility and I have no idea what to do with him, or for that matter, for him. I don't know what to do with a kid. I can't even keep myself straight without an assistant." She realized she was screaming at him and took a deep breath. "I'm going home now. If he doesn't want me, then I guess there isn't a damn thing I can do to make him go with me."

"Simply love him." She looked up when she realized she was sobbing again and the man was gone. She stood there for several minutes before she moved out of the building and into the fresh air.

There were things she had to do, things that needed done now. Sitting on the long low wall, she let the breeze blow over her, almost feeling as if it were taking away some of the pressure she suddenly found herself under. When she opened her eyes, the list she needed to get done seemed complete and she pulled out her phone.

She had to get arrangements made. Dusty knew that her sister had made funeral arrangements along with her will, but not what they were. There were people to call and make sure her nephew was going to be well. Dusty wasn't sure what happened now, and told herself she didn't want him any more than he did her, but she knew that for the lie that it was. She wanted him in her life, if for nothing but the simply reason he was all she had left.

Sitting there for a few more minutes, Dusty knew two things. She was more alone than she'd ever been, and as of right now, she was as depressed as she ever would be again. Standing, she re-entered the hospital. The sooner she was finished with this, the quicker she could get moving again.

# Chapter 1

Galin sat in the hall just outside the offices and waited. It was his turn next and he dreaded this more than he had anything. They were going to marry him off and he had no desire for it to happen. But what did one say to a man like Boss? His word was law.

"Galin? Would you like to come in now?" He wanted to tell Michael no, but stood and nodded. *Might as well get it over with*, he thought. Moving through the great doors, he was shown to a large table and asked to have a seat. The file appeared in front of him before he could ask any questions.

"This boy you are going to protect is somewhat of a problem child. He has had a great deal thrown at him, but—"

"Boy?" Boss nodded and frowned. "No, I'm sorry, but it should be a woman, not a boy. I'm not...you're going to assign me my wife to care for. I don't want one, but I know it should be female. What is this about?" He pushed the file back at Michael.

"You want a wife? It was my understanding that you have no wish to be wed. Am I correct on that?" Galin nodded and looked at the file with the picture of a young boy on it. He appeared to be in his early teens maybe, but he wasn't much older than that. "Galin? Do you wish for me to reassign you? Do you have no desire to help this young man?"

"I thought I was going into the rotation to find me a wife. The way that you did for Riss and Agon." He looked up at Boss and Michael, who had summoned him today. "I had thought that the Mystic's were a way for you to get rid of us all, and marrying us off was better than having us die. I'm...I'm not sure what's going on now."

"I do not wish for anyone to die, Galin. But you have expressed a desire to not wed, and I do listen to the men and woman who work for me." Galin thought Boss was angry, but wasn't really sure so he said nothing. "Would you like to go over this file? Or do you wish to come back later? He is in a rough way, this young man, but he can wait for another time."

"Now. I'm ready now." He was both disappointed and relieved by not being matched to a female. He wasn't ready to settle down, and he had a feeling that a woman would take away his ability to do what he loved most. He was a fun man, and those around him had always come to him when they needed cheering up. He looked at Michael when he started to explain what was needed.

"His name is Kipling McGee, but he goes by Kip. He is living with his aunt now, but they are both most unhappy with their forced arrangements. The aunt's name is Dusty McGee; she, like his mother, was...is...single. The young man is very...his mother was killed a month ago and he has been living with the aunt, as I have said. Things are not going well for the young man and he will need a great deal from you, I'm afraid. More than someone you might have been with for a long while. His temper is short and he has taken to skipping school, as well as hanging with the wrong crowd. You will need to work hard at having him listen to you. He has shut us all out."

"His mother is dead? How did this happen?" He looked up when neither man answered him. "She took her own life?"

"Nay," Boss said to him with a sad shake to his head. "She was in an accident in which she was said to be at fault. There were others involved but all were fine. Miss McGee was driving to an appointment and using her phone. She hit another car and was pushed into the intersection and hit several more times before she stopped. Her injuries were profound and she did not live long. The son and sister were there when she was pronounced. There was already a great deal of bad blood between the three of them, and now there is more. I do believe the boy…he will not survive if he is not taken to task soon. He is going down a path that will not see him live long, I'm afraid."

Galin looked at the several pictures of the young man. There was one of him and his mother, and three more of him smiling. The last two were of him looking angry, and one of him looking lost. This one Galin knew was the true child, and his heart broke for him.

"I would ask that you observe him for several days to see what you can work with. Most of the time he is locked away in his room, but he does come out when he believes there is no one about. Tread carefully with this boy, Galin. He is very fragile right now." He looked up when Michael cleared his throat before continuing. "His last protector…his last protector has disappeared. We think that Markum has returned."

"You mean since he was at Judith and Agon's place?" Michael nodded and Galin looked at Boss. "Why now? I mean, what does he think he can do after all these decades? Surely you don't think that he's done something with…you do, don't you?"

"Just after Kip's mother was in her accident, a flurry of messages came from Gordon, the young man's protector. Short things as in 'trouble,' 'damage.' I had no way of contacting him then, as he suddenly disappeared from my radar as soon as I received them. Then nothing. I tried several times to find him to reach out to see what was happening, but he never returned any of my calls or came to me." Boss looked so afraid that Galin felt his own fear start to rise. "You will watch the boy, please? I don't know if Gordon will contact you, but he might reach out to the young man."

"He can do that?" Boss nodded at him but said nothing more.

"I'll keep an eye on him. But I have to wonder, why would Markum want Gordon? He is young in comparison to the other protectors, and has little experience in dealing with the kind of evil that Markum would use."

"That is precisely why he'd contact him. His lack of experience and his young age makes him a perfect person to contact. It's also why he would be easier prey for one such as Markum." Galin looked down at the pictures again as Boss continued. "Or he may want to hurt us through the child. Who knows with one such as him?"

Galin left a few minutes later and made his way to his newest charge. He was right where Michael had told him he'd be, holed up in his bedroom with the music blaring. Galin watched him from the corner of his room nearest his ceiling and wondered what was going through his mind.

Galin noticed that his computer was on and moved to see the screen.

At first he wasn't sure what he was looking at. When the image of a can of soup with crackers started to move about, he realized it was an advertisement. As he had an idea that Kip wouldn't be watching commercials, he waited for the thing to end and whatever it was he was watching to appear. As soon as the commercial for the crackers — as it turned out to be — disappeared, Kip typed in another search. This time an image of a child watching something on a small computer appeared.

"Stupid, stupid, stupid." Galin stepped back from the venom in Kip's voice and watched him carefully. "She thinks I don't know what she's doing all day. There is no way she's making money off this crap."

He watched as Kip pulled up three more commercials. Each one he derailed for its stupidity as well as calling them "lame" and "retarded." Whatever was going on with the woman he was upset about, Galin didn't see what had upset the boy. When someone knocked at his door, both he and Kip turned to it when a voice sounded from the other side.

"Kip, dinner is ready. Come on out and eat." When Kip stood up, Galin did as well. But instead of going out to eat, Kip simply turned the music up louder before sitting down again. Galin knew then that this was going to be his aunt.

*You should get something to eat. There is no need for you to go hungry when someone has fixed you a meal.* Galin knew that he'd heard him but all he did was shake his head. *Kip, aren't you hungry? It's late and you need to keep your strength up. Please, go do as you've been asked.*

Kip opened a drawer in his desk and pulled out three large candy bars. As he peeled one open, Galin laughed a little at the stubbornness of the young. Of course he'd have a stash. Galin did as well in his own place. But the boy was hurting by not interacting with people, while Galin would eat in his room to continue playing one of his many gaming systems.

This went on for over two hours, with Kip stealing a candy bar from his drawer and pulling up commercial after commercial on his computer. After Kip fell asleep on the bed with a book on his chest, Galin shifted from his world to that of the boy and looked around.

As far as rooms went it looked like every other child's room he'd ever been in. There were clothes laying on the floor that were either dirty or clean, depending on the pile. The bed looked as if he had not made it in days. The closet door hung open and hangers looked like they were giving a high-five to the clothing that had ended up laying over a few pairs of shoes. The walls were a bright blue, Galin thought, because he could see very little of them. Instead, the walls were mostly covered in what looked like graffiti and drawn on with pens and crayons, with a total disregard for the person who owned the house. Perhaps that was the point. The boy — young man he supposed — was more than just upset with his aunt. He was angry with the world in general.

Some things on the desk made Galin think that whoever Kip's aunt was, she was not giving him whatever the boy wanted. He found references to her not supplying him with the boots he wanted, nor tickets to some football game at the school. Galin also found a notepad of all the things that she'd spent money on.

One list was marked "unnecessary" and another was labeled "superfluous." These two lists seemed to say the same thing, but the things on them were funny to him. Haircut and car were just two of the superfluous things. The unnecessary list contained things like stockings and maid service. The latter made Galin take a look around the room again, thinking that was a definite necessity, especially for this room. Spending the day with the boy proved to be both exhausting and enlightening. The young man did need help.

When his replacement showed up for the sleep duty, Galin went to his own room and sat down on the couch. He looked around his rooms and realized that he needed to clean up after himself a little more. A knock at his door had him bidding the person enter, and he sat up straighter when Michael came in.

"I have that file for you. I thought you could use some more information on the child." Galin took it and waited for whatever else that Michael wanted, and he could tell there was more. "I should like for you to tell me something. It's about the woman, Kip's aunt. Have you any interaction with her protector?"

"I didn't even see the aunt at all but spent the day observing the boy. He is...the boy is most troubled, Michael. Someone came to the door once to tell Kip dinner was ready, but he didn't leave the room and I didn't either." Michael nodded. "Is her protector gone as well?"

"Oh no. I was just...she's with Jacob. He said that she was...he worries about her some. He thinks she is not doing well." Galin could understand that. He didn't have any sisters or brothers by blood, but he had lost a great many people he'd come to love like one. "He has been with her since birth and he has noticed a great deal of things lately. Some of them are not...it is most worrisome for him."

"I know that Kip is mad at her. He has these lists of things that she has denied him. Things that he feels she has purchased for herself that he thinks are not useful or cost worthy. Could that have a little to do with it?" Michael shrugged. "I could see if he would cut her some slack, as I've heard said. I don't think he's been doing that. Of course, she could be just as bad as he believes, too."

"Please see what you can do about him helping her, or at the very least communicating with her on some level." Galin nodded and waited again. "There is something else. I was wondering if you would do me a favor. Not a large one, mind you, but one all the same. I need something from...Judith has given me a jar of some of her exquisite jelly and I've no bread to eat it on. I know that you have partaken of some of the foods on earth and may have run across this bread called sourdough. I should like to try it."

"Sure, but I don't think that's something you want to eat jam on. It's more of a sandwich bread. Kind of has a bite to it." Michael nodded. "I can get you some, but I think you'd enjoy it more on a biscuit, or even some toast."

Michael left him a few minutes later after deciding that he did want the bread, but he'd take some biscuits as well. After going over the file again Galin decided to go to bed. He'd have to get up earlier with a school-aged charge, and he wanted to be there when he woke up.

~~~

Kip waited until he was sure that his aunt had left for work before leaving his room. He really hated her and was going to make her suffer every minute she did him by keeping him here. Why they'd had to move to her house instead of just staying at the one his mom and him had was beyond him. It wasn't like she had a real job or anything, and she seemed to always have money to burn. When she did leave for this so called job, she more than likely just sat around all day eating those fancy cookies she liked and drinking coffee. And probably having sex on the desk with her boss.

Frowning, Kip amended his complaints about his aunt. "She doesn't even own a coffee maker, so she probably buys that crap at the shop with an 'e' on the end of it. Like the word 'shoppe' makes a whole lot of difference." He giggled a little at his own joke but sobered quickly. He felt guilty laughing and tried hard not to do it. But he had noticed that it was becoming harder every day.

When he figured out the kitchen was empty of her and that stupid little case she carried around, he looked around the cabinets, trying to find something to eat. He'd have to restore his supply soon or he'd have to come out and have a meal with her. Last night his belly had thought his throat was cut. Man, he was starving. Kip found a can of soup in the back of one of her cabinets and dumped it into a bowl that was on the counter.

The rest of her house was nice and clean. The cleaning lady he'd met one day when he skipped school had been about to go into his room, but he'd told her it was off limits to everyone and had gone out and bought a lock that night. Now no one could go into his little space unless he let them. Smiling, he thought of what Dusty had said about his room on his first day there.

"You can have your own space. All I ask is that you keep it clean and that you don't mark up the walls. I want to sell this in a few years and I don't really want to spend a great deal on repairs, all right?" Of course the first thing he'd done was take out his pocket knife and cut the date into the wall, and had been making hash marks every day since. It had only been twenty-three days, but it seemed an eternity. When the timer beeped on the microwave, he sat at the table with a spoon to eat.

His mother was dead. Some days he'd think about it and would have to find a quiet dark place and bawl like a little baby. It wasn't like she'd never left him alone. There were times when she'd be gone for three or four days at a time, and only returned long enough then to get some clean cloths and leave him a few bucks before she left him again. But this time was different. She was never coming back.

Shoving the bowl back, he thought about her laying there in the hospital. Her head looked like someone had wrapped her in pink rags, and her body, what he could see of it, was black and blue. But the machines and wires they had on her were what had terrified him. There were so many beeps and dings coming from them that he hated going in there to see her. But he did. Because his hope was—and he still had it—that she'd come out of this. That she'd wake up and tell him things were fine.

The doctors had told Dusty that his mom was clinically dead. That there had been so much damage done to her head and body that if she did live, it would not be a quality of life that would be good for any of them. He had no idea what that meant, but Dusty had said that his mom had a DNR paper signed. He asked her what that meant after the doctor left them.

"It means that nothing heroic is to be done if she dies. She told me a long time ago, just after you were born, that she didn't want to live on life support…that we were to end her life if it came to that. Our dad was on life support

26

for three months before Mom finally let him go. I think that's why your mom wanted this. It's hard on people. And she would never have wanted that." Kip had stood up and towered over his aunt when she finished.

"So you're going to okay them letting her die? She's my mom. And your sister. How the hell can you just let them kill her like that?" She started to speak but he cut her off. "You go and tell them right now you changed your mind. I can't live without my mom. And I won't be living with you."

"You most certainly will be living with me." When she stood up he took a step back. When his mom looked at him like that, she usually followed it up with a punch to the face, but all Dusty did was take a deep breath. "I know that you're hurting right now. So am I, but we have to do what is best for your mom. You heard the doctor. She won't be able to survive on her own. She'll be hooked up to something to make her heart beat and her lungs function. Her brain function is gone, Kip. Your mother is gone."

He stormed away from her and decided that no matter what, she was not going to take him from his mother. Yet here he was, sitting in her house with nothing of his own except for a few pairs of pants and his backpack. And all his other things…Dusty had told him that they were gone.

"How can my things be gone?" he asked his now cold soup. "I had it all in the apartment. She just was too lazy to go and get it for me. And she wouldn't even let me stick around and say goodbye to my friends. Now look at me. I'm stuck in this house with no one and nothing. And I hate her more than I ever did anybody else."

Kip went back to his room, thankful that it was Saturday. He thought about cleaning it up—he was having a hard time finding things in it—but only picked up his clothes. He took them all to the little laundry room and put in a load while he tried to decide what else to do with his day. It would be easy enough to avoid his aunt, but that game was getting boring.

Dusty would work until about five today. She'd mentioned on the flight back from his home that she had this big project to get finished and then she'd not be so busy. He barely listened to her and couldn't have told anybody what she'd said most of the trip back to her place if someone would have asked. Instead he tried to think of ways to get back at her.

She'd taken him to a department store to get him some clothes on the first day. He didn't want them, but knew that if he didn't pick out some things, she'd do it for him. And he didn't want to be thought of as a frigging nerd. The way she dressed, all fancy and shit, was bad enough. There was no way he was going to be caught wearing what he knew was going to be sweater vests and dress pants. So he'd gotten three pair of pants and four shirts. She'd made him get some underwear too, and a coat. He'd never had a winter coat before, just a jacket that his mom would get from the free drive at the beginning of fall. And none of them had ever fit him like this one did. When the wash was finished, Kip put in another load and put the wet things in the dryer.

He'd been caring for himself for a long time. His mother, even when she was home, rarely did more than talk on her cell phone when she had service, or watch television when they had that. And her idea of a hot meal was having the pizza guy come to the house with their food rather than her going to get it and bringing it back. Most of the time, he'd end up eating alone while his mom "paid" the guy with a trip to her bedroom.

Kip wasn't as stupid as some people thought he was. He knew they also thought his mother was a bad mother. Most of the time, he thought so too. The electric only stayed on because it was included in the rent. Cable would be on for a few months after she'd get her taxes done, then the money would be gone and so would the cable. They had food at the beginning of the month, but nothing by the end because she'd use the food card to buy steaks and crap for her boyfriends. And the apartment they lived in had rats bigger than cats and smelled like people peed in it all the time. In the summer months it was nearly impossible to sleep with the windows closed because the smell would heat up and it would be nasty. But she'd been his mom. The only one he'd ever have.

When his laundry was finished he took it to his room, and when he saw what a mess it all was he stripped down his bed and put his sheets in the washer as well. By the time they were washed and dried he'd been able to get his room in better shape and had three bags of trash to show for it. Ashamed he'd let it get that bad, he put the bags in the trashcan in the back of the house and even took out the kitchen trash. But he made sure he was in his room again when Dusty came home at six-thirty.

Dusty came to his door twice. Once she asked him to come to dinner, the second time she'd begged him to let her in. He'd had to turn the music up twice as loud when she started crying. He didn't want her tears to make him sad, but they did, especially when she told him that she missed his mom too. Kip wanted to tell her it was her fault that she wasn't there, but said nothing. By midnight, he was in bed and trying to sleep.

The dream started off like the others he'd had about his mom. She was in the hospital bed all banged up, but this time he saw a man standing next to her. He looked at Kip. The smile he gave him made Kip want to take a hot shower, but he stood still. It was a dream after all, and no one could hurt you in dreams.

"I've taken her." The man came toward him and stopped just short of touching him. "You look so much like her that I want to take you as well. I can't just yet. But soon. Especially on the path you're on."

"Who are you?" The man moved back to the bed and touched his mom's cheek, and the monitor started beeping. But when he moved away, the machine settled again. Kip was so confused that he tried to work things out, only to end up with a pain in his head. His mother was dead and yet this man was with her somehow. "I asked you a question. Who are you?"

"I have many names. And many looks. Would you like to see the one I like the best?" Kip nodded before he thought about it and the room seemed to catch fire, the heat was so intense.

The man...shifted was all Kip could think to call it. One minute he was standing there looking like a normal person and the next...the next had Kip screaming when he touched his leg. As soon as he opened his eyes someone came near him and he threw out his fists. It wasn't until the light came on that he realized he'd hit his aunt, and Kip was sure as shit he'd killed her.

# Chapter 2

If she had to tell one more person she was all right she might just pull out a gun and shoot the lot of them. If she'd owned a gun she might have hurt Kip when she went rushing into his room when he'd screamed, and that would have been bad. Looking at her nephew, she wondered if he'd ever like her. Denise handed her a Baggie of ice as a man came toward them.

"Miss McGee, can you tell us again why your son hit you?" She eyed the man, wondering if she could hit him and get away with it. He flushed brightly and she had a feeling he could see she was pissed. "It's just that you —"

"It's her nephew, and I believe she's told you that nearly two dozen times. Now, unless you want me to pound you in the head with that book you're holding, I would suggest you step back." The man nodded at Denise so hard that his glasses fell down on his nose and nearly off his face. When he backed off, a man in a suit sat down. Dusty pulled the ice pack from her face.

"I will hurt you if you ask me the same questions again. I'm in no mood to fuck with you people any longer. I'm not even sure how the hell you all got here." He nodded and looked at Kip when he shouted. "I think it's time you people left us alone. You've seen to my wound, and as I have said countless times, he didn't mean it. He had a bad dream. Understandable if you knew what was going on, but it's time to go."

"You know that when he called the police he told them he'd killed you." She nodded. Kip had been standing over her with the phone in his hand when she'd woken up. He told her he'd called the cops and the number over the phone. It was why Denise had come barreling in before the police arrived. "We have to treat this like we would any other domestic disturbance."

"And how is this the same as a man beating his wife or the other way around? I startled him into reacting. Frankly, I'm quite proud of him for being able to defend himself. It makes me feel better knowing that he's —"

"Did you know that he's burnt?" She stood up and started for Kip when the man stopped her. "You'll upset him if you ask him about it, and he looks ready to explode right now." Dusty turned to look at him. "I swear to you as soon as the cops leave, I'll have a look at it myself. My wife is on her way here and she wants to see it."

"Why?" He nodded toward the chair. "Okay then. You know me but I don't have a clue who the hell you are or why that cop looks ready to piss himself every time you look his way. So if your wife wants to see Kip, then you'd better do some major explaining. Or you're going to have a majorly pissed off woman on your hands and trust me, I'm not a piece of fluff."

"I'm Commissioner Anderson. Benny to my friends. You're…you won't believe me when I tell you what I suspect happened to your nephew, so we'll leave it for —"

"Get out." Dusty had had enough. "I want all of you to get out of my house right now. You don't want to explain, I don't want you here. So pack your stuff, and leave."

"I'm not human." Dusty stopped moving toward the door when Benny spoke from behind her. "I know you believe me. You have two people working for you that aren't human as well. I'd very much like to explain, but right now I don't have enough information to give you, and what I suspect will scare the shit out of you."

Dusty sat down but not near Benny this time. She watched the other men leave her, and then Kip get up and go to his room. He'd not said a single word to her since he'd told her he was sorry he'd hurt her. He'd not even told her he had been hurt or what the dream he'd had was about. When she'd asked, he shut her out like he had for the past few weeks. An hour later Denise left too, telling her that she'd rearrange her meetings in the morning so she could come in later.

"He hates me." Benny didn't say anything, for which she was grateful. "His mom was in a car accident about a month ago and was killed. Kip is pissed at me because I'm the only one left to take care of him. His mother and I...we didn't actually get along very well, and when she moved out, I moved on. I had to, or else be sucked into whatever mess she'd get herself into the next time, then the next. I don't know what she ever told him about me, but I'm assuming he has no idea that I bailed his mom out more than she did herself. He thinks...Kip thinks that I killed her because she had a DNR in place."

"I'm sorry for your loss." She nodded and reached for a tissue from the box he held out. "Have you told him everything?"

Dusty looked at Benny with a frown. "I don't know what you mean. He was there, he knows that she's gone and that I'm taking care of him."

"When you brought him here we were notified that he had a minor record and that his mother had one as well. Hers was...extensive and varied. Most of it should have put her in prison. We're required to notify other districts when someone comes into our town with any kind of criminal record. Along with his file and that of his mother, we were given the run down on everything that happened when she died. That includes the things that were sold off for collections." Benny handed her a large envelope. "This came to me today. It's an accounting of what was sold and how much more you owe. I'm so sorry."

Dusty didn't even look at it. She'd gotten the same thing yesterday. "I had to empty my savings account to pay for the hospital bills before they'd let me have her body for burial. And the funeral home said I had to pay up front because they knew of her...circumstances. The police had been very busy while she was dying making sure that everyone knew that if they wanted anything from the estate, they'd better be tapping into me as soon as possible. Then to fly us both back home and to purchase Kip something to wear was...."

"Expensive." She nodded and wiped her tears. She hated crying and she'd been doing a lot of it lately. "You should let him know. All of it. How you've sold most everything that means even the slightest bit to you so that you could raise him properly. More than likely, this is the first real home and family he's had. No offense to your sister. But perhaps he'll realize how lucky he is."

"No. I don't...his mom left him for days on end the cops told me. Days and days without as much as a nickel to his name. How the hell could she do that to her own child? And then when I brought him home, he told me that his mom had told him that I'd never helped her in all the years we'd been apart. She apparently told him that I had hurt her somehow and had washed my hands of them both long ago." She laughed bitterly. "I paid their rent for two years before I found out she didn't even live in the building any longer. The landlord had been splitting the rent money I sent him with her. That's when I decided she'd have to get a job on her own. I just didn't know it would be as a mule for some drug lord. And because of the food stamp fraud against her, I can't even get any help for Kip. None whatsoever. My sister might be dead, Commissioner Anderson, but she is still fucking up my life and his from the grave."

She was broke. Not really broke, she amended, but personally she had nothing more to fall back on. The business she owned was in great condition, in the black for the last five years. But she'd never borrow from the company. Right now, it was her only support, and Kip's. And if things went the way she thought they would in a few months, she was going to be fucked there as well. Things were not going as she'd...it was going down the tubes and she was quickly going with it, thanks to her landlords and the fact that they were going to run her out of business by jacking up the rent. If it were just her, she'd sell out and try to find something else, but she had Kip and she'd never let him do without again.

"My wife." Dusty stood up, embarrassed that she never heard the door open. Benny nodded at the woman by his side as he made the introductions. "Dusty McGee, I'd like you to meet my wife, Lily Anderson. She isn't human either."

"I got that." As soon as Lily put out her hand, Dusty hesitated. "I've heard that touching someone can give more than you want them to have. While I don't want to be rude, I don't know what you are or how you'd use it again me. My life is in the toilet enough, thanks."

"I understand. I have been watching you for a few hours. I was once a protector. I know you have no idea what that is, but I will explain." She looked over her shoulder and smiled. "This is your protector. His name is Jacob."

The man seemed to fade into the room and Dusty took a step back. She watched as he spread wings out but never moved toward her. When she looked at Lily again, she too had wings, as did Benny. Dusty didn't so much sit down as she fell into the chair behind her. Things were just going clickety click too fast.

"I'm not sleeping, am I? I mean, this is not all a dream where in a few hours my alarm will sound and I'll wake up thinking what a strange dream I've had. Or nightmare. I can handle a nightmare. I certainly have enough of them." Jacob shook his head and his wings disappeared. "Are you around all the time? I mean, like all the time?"

"Most of the time I am. Not when you sleep. There is someone, a night protector, who comes to you then while I rest. I do not sleep, but I do need to rest." She nodded, not sure what to say to him. "Are you going to scream?"

"I'm not a screamer." He nodded and sat down. "How long have you been here? I mean watching…protecting me?"

"Since you were born. I was assigned to you for your life and will bring you over when you have finished with this one." She nodded again, terrified beyond words. "I shall not harm you, Dusty. I am here only to protect you.

36

We all wish to only protect, but things have happened here and we must have you aware of us. It is much worse than you have even imagined."

She thought of times when she'd felt someone was with her but never really…. "I just need a minute here. A few…maybe a few days. My sister, she had one too? Where was he when she needed him?"

"Your sister was…her protector tried to help her. She would not…there were times when he was only able to keep her from death by calling in help. Rose was not…she was her own worst enemy." Dusty couldn't argue with that so said nothing more to Jacob. Lily smiled at her before she spoke.

"I should like to see the mark on your nephew's leg. I will not disturb him, but I must look. If it is as we think, then I will speak to you about it and explain what will need to be done." Dusty nodded and Lily faded from the room. In a few seconds she was back, and she looked afraid. Dusty stood up, wondering what had happened to Kip now. "He is sleeping. His protector has helped him sleep and he will rest for a while. He is…Kip has been touched by a demi-god."

The room seemed to fill with people. They didn't come in the front door like regular people did, but sort of just appeared. She knew she had to talk to them, had to find out how to protect Kip, but it was too much. They were too much.

Dusty got up and walked to the kitchen. She had no idea why she had to get away, but she needed air. The house was suddenly devoid of it. Going out onto the tiny deck, she stood there without a coat just making herself breathe in and out. When someone leaned against the railing next to her, she simply glanced over but said nothing.

"I am called Boss." Dusty didn't care if His name was God, and looked at Him again when He laughed. "You will have questions for me, I'm sure. I can answer all that you ask, but I will be truthful with my answers. So if you do not wish to truly know, do not ask."

"I don't even know where to begin. There are…there are…." She looked out over the yard. "I don't know what is going on. I'm freaking out a…there are winged people in my living room, my nephew has been touched by a demi-god, I've had this man watching over me since I was a baby, and right now all I can do is make myself breathe in and out. So pardon me all to hell if I need just a minute, all right?"

"I'm sorry for that. But we must protect young Kipling more than ever now. What we have feared has happened. Someone has marked him, and with the emotions that Kipling is going through right now, the man may harm all of us before he is finished." She looked at him, wanting to ask but afraid to. "Yes, he will kill the boy before he is finished if we do not work now to save him."

Dusty didn't say anything. She didn't even know what she would say if she could. There was only so much a person could take in and she was pretty sure she was at her limit…maybe even over the weight load for something like this. She flushed when she thought of the shower she'd taken before bed. Boss laughed again.

"He does not join you in the bath. He simply watches over you. You are not to fear him because you know that he is there now." Dusty snorted. "That is a habit a friend of mine has. When she is…disbelieving something I have said to her, she snorts like that. My friend Michael, he does it as well. He, however, is trying to break the habit."

"If You give her the bullshit You just did me, then I can understand." She sat in one of the chairs on her deck and shivered. As suddenly as she realized she was cold, she was warmed. When she looked at the man with her, He simply shrugged. As much as she wanted to ask, she didn't want to know even more if He had warmed her up. "Why Kip?"

"There are many reasons I could give you, but none will satisfy you. I should like to talk to you about what has happened before this. Jacob thinks that you are upset with him because your sister has passed." Dusty didn't answer but He didn't seem to need her to. "She was ready. I know that is hard to think of now, but things must go along as they should, and though you do not understand them, it is important for the pieces to fall into place to move forward. It is a timeline, you call it, a schedule of events. Thing fall into place in the order they are needed to be."

"I call it bullshit." He looked startled at her but didn't say anything as she continued. "Free will. I have it. My sister had it, and I'm sure everyone has it. She had a free will to do what she did, and I think someone should have been there to guide her differently. Why didn't they? You're supposed to protect her…where was her protector when she was selling dope? Taking drugs and leaving her only child to fend for himself? Answer me that."

He sat down across from her and she had a feeling He was going to be angry with her. Instead, He stretched out his feet and smiled. "When you were seventeen years old you were set on leaving home and taking up with a man that was twice your age who said he wanted to help you with your career."

"He said that I had talent. I suppose he was right, but I now realize it was just sex he wanted. I had talent all the same, just not what he was talking about. Are You saying that I should have chosen the other path, the one that had me going with him?" Boss shook his head. "Then what? You're making no sense to me right now."

"You were to do just as you wished. Had you gone with him in his adventure you would have ended up in the same place you are now, but you would have been much less successful and a great deal poorer. Not just in money, but in trust as well. He would have hardened you for that." Dusty didn't really trust a great many people now and had a hard time believing she could trust less. "You would have been much like a hermit, I think. Working from your home and never leaving it to interact with customers. It would have made you some money, but not enough to support you and young Kipling."

"You can tell me if he ever comes to love me." He nodded. "Does he? Do you think he'll ever come to love me, just a little? I love him. It's hard, really hard sometimes, but I do love him. He's all I have left of my sister, all I have left of anything really."

"He loves you now, Dusty. He just isn't sure what to do about it." She stared at him for several seconds before she looked out over the yard again. She'd had so many plans for her home. The building she'd been about to buy downtown had been next on her list of things to do. The rent she was paying was killing her and she'd never own it. And if the new owners of her building were going to raise her rent again, she'd have to move out, find something cheaper, maybe in some part of town she didn't want to be in during the day, much less at night. Now that too was put on hold. Stiffening her spine, she looked over at the man only to discover He was gone. Dusty sat there for several more minutes before she moved into the house. It was time to get things done. Sunday was her only day off and she didn't think she'd get any sleep anyway.

~~~

Galin watched the boy sleep. It was well past noon and the aunt had gone out several minutes ago, but had knocked on the door to tell Kip she was leaving. Galin had wanted to tell her not to wake the boy but she'd left before he was disturbed.

He looked down at the scar on Kip's leg and felt a new kind of fear. When he'd summoned Benny to the house it had been for him to look at the wound, but Kip had refused to let him near him. Galin had finally suggested that Kip was exhausted and had him go to bed. Lily had confirmed what he had already thought. Kip had been marked.

"What will happen to him now?" He knew that Michael was nearby and didn't even bother reaching for him when he asked. "I'm worried for him. I cannot leave him now that Markum has come here. I won't let anything else happen to him. It's bad enough that his aunt ignores him so much."

"You think that she ignores him, Galin?" He nodded. "Hmm. I have not known her well, but I think that she loves the boy and worries for him. The way she talked to Benny about him last evening makes me think she would kill for the child. He is much loved, my good friend. But the boy has to let it in before you can see it, I think."

"She treats him poorly. He is locked in here all day when he isn't at school. Did you know that he eats candy bars rather than a balanced meal? Why isn't she making him come out to have something good to eat with her? She certainly eats well." Galin had no idea if she ate or not, but he was upset that he'd not been there for Kip when Markum had come for him. "What sort of person is she? No better than his mother, I think. And that is sad to me."

"I think perhaps you are forgetting that there are two sides to every story. Mayhap you are only hearing the one that Kip wants you to know. Have you met Dusty as yet? She is a very lonely woman who is trying her best to make this work. And at great expense to herself. Dusty has given up so much to give this boy a home, a roof over his head, and food that he chooses not to eat. She will wear out soon if he does not give in." Galin glanced at the bed and wondered why he'd taken such a dislike to someone he'd never met. "You should encourage him to meet her halfway. The woman is hurting as well."

"She does what she will and leaves him to his own devices all day and night. What can she be doing that would take her from home so much?" Michael said nothing but Galin didn't care. "I should think she would be here with him. Making sure that he knows he isn't alone. Had I the ability, I would speak to him all the time, tell him that I love him and am here for him. What has she done?"

Michael said nothing as he moved about the room. It was clean now, or at least in better shape than it had been the first day. And his clothing was now hanging on hangers instead of lying about. When Michael stopped at the desk and looked at the computer, Galin flushed. He could not discourage the boy from looking at some of the sites he'd been looking at.

"He is curious about sex, which is understandable. Perhaps you could guide him in a more...safe part of his education. All lovemaking does not involve paddles or whips." Galin said nothing, thinking that he'd never seen such pictures in his life and didn't know why his body had responded like it had when he'd seen them. But he had been telling Kip to go to other sites, ones that talked of love and romance.

"I have something I wish for you to do." Galin, happy for the change of subject, agreed to it. "You may want to hear what it is first. I don't know if you will like me much for my request."

"I shall do whatever it takes to get the boy the help he needs. Tell me what you need of me and I'll do it." Michael nodded and ran his finger along the scar on Kip's leg. Instead of the large handprint that had been there, now it was only a small mark. Galin knew that Michael, even as strong as he was, couldn't remove it completely.

"I want you to go and spend some time with Dusty. Not a great deal, mind you, but you need to know what she is up to as well if you are to help the boy. Right now you are only hearing all that she has done to him from the young man. But not what she has done for him that he is not aware of. It might help you." Galin had thought that too. But in order for him to spend time with the aunt, he'd have to leave Kip unattended. Not something he wanted to do in light of recent events. "I shall watch him for a few hours. And I believe Riss has asked to help as well."

"I don't think it will help matters much. She has her own protector." Galin looked at Kip again as he continued. "I fear for him. I should have been here for him but I was not. Now he will bear this mark until something is done about Markum."

Michael sat down on the bed and stared at him. Galin knew he was telling him to get lost, a phrase that his last charge had said a great deal. But he was loath to do so. To leave would mean that he wasn't able to protect Kip again. But Michael nodded to the door and Galin stood up. He moved to the door to slip out of the room when he looked back at Michael.

"You will call me if he needs me?" Michael said he would. "I don't want to leave him. I have grown quite fond of him in the past few days. He has suffered a great deal for someone so young."

"So has his aunt." Galin didn't want to believe that and wasn't sure why. His negative feelings for this unknown woman had him feeling guilty more than he'd ever been. "You will spend the day with her and come back tonight. I have some free time and if I do not, I will call for Riss or Agon. Each of them will watch him as you would."

Galin knew that in his mind but not his heart. He wanted to stay but knew that arguing would not get him anywhere with Michael. Galin moved out of the room and into the hall, where he saw her. Dusty McGee was not what he had expected.

He'd already figured out she was younger than most aunts he'd encountered lately. But to his thinking she'd still be older than she looked to be right now. With her sweatpants on and her tee shirt rolled up at the sleeves, she looked to be about sixteen. He thought if she let her pony tail down it might add a few years but not much.

*She is twenty-seven. Younger than her sister was by eight years.* He didn't say anything to Boss when He spoke to him. *This is a good thing that you are doing. You should know the person who cares so lovingly for your charge. Dusty is a good woman.*

44

*He doesn't like her much.* Boss said nothing so Galin continued. *He doesn't seem to think she gives him all that he needs. And there are things from his past that she wouldn't let him keep.*

*There are many things you are not aware of, Galin. Nor is the child. Dusty did what she could to get his things for him, but the courts said that she had to leave them. They are to be sold at auction so the people that Rose owed money to may recoup some of their losses.* Boss appeared to him just as he followed Dusty to the kitchen. *She has paid what she could, but there simply was too much money owed to a great many people. Then there are the hospital bills, the funeral arrangements, the cost to bring young Kipling here, the clothing he now has. Things are mounting up for the young woman. And she bears this all on her own, not wanting to tarnish his idea of his mother. Even now she has someone going to the sale to get what she can, even at great cost to herself.*

The woman moved around the kitchen, pulling out things from the refrigerator and wiping them down. He watched her for several minutes as she then cleaned the shelves before putting all the items back inside. She was also writing things down, and he walked over to her list. On the top of the paper was a list of the candy bars that Kip had eaten, as well as the cans of soup the boy had taken from the kitchen. She knew, was all he could think. The woman knew that Kip was living on candy bars to avoid her.

Several times she went to the door to knock. The first two times she'd not gotten a response, but the third time the music came blasting from the other side, telling them both that Kip was awake. Galin watched her lean against the wall and cry for ten minutes, and his heart melted some for her. When she went to her room for an hour, he nearly followed her but she came out dressed to go out.

Her stopping at Kip's door had him slipping into the room.

"I'm going to the grocery. Do you need anything?" No answer, but Kip did look at the door. "You can even come with me if you want."

A few seconds passed and neither of them said anything else, and Galin went out of the room again. He sat beside her in the car as she drove, sobbing the entire way to the store.

Galin felt sorry for them both. Two of the most stubborn people he knew were in the same house and neither of them was giving an inch. He decided that he needed to do something for them and tried to think what. Reaching for Kala and Judith, he asked them to meet him later at the house. Both agreed, and he wasn't surprised at all to see Judith at the store when they got there. He nodded to the woman he was watching and learning about.

"Hello." Judith smiled at Dusty before pulling out a cart as well. "I've seen you around town. Are you the lady who owns Strategize? The advertising firm?"

"I am." Galin smiled when Judith winked at him when Dusty answered her. "You need something? I'm not taking on any big clients right now but perhaps I can find...I know you own Jellies, Jams, and Preserves, right? I'd like to work with you, but right now...well, right now I'm not sure I can handle a client as big as you're going to be."

"Thanks. And yes you can. And you will." Judith moved her cart alongside of Dusty's, talking a mile a minute, telling her what she wanted from Dusty in advertising. It sounded to Galin like Judith had it all worked out on her own, but talked to Dusty like it was a done deal.

And so a friendship, albeit a working one, began. Galin watched as Judith did what he was sure hadn't happened in a great long time for Dusty. He watched her smile.

# Chapter 3

On the way home from the store Dusty stopped at the new shop that Judith had opened. She was jealous of what the other woman had been able to do in such a short amount of time, and even looked longingly at the building next to JJ&P, as Judith called her shop for short. By the time she pulled up in front of the building, Dusty had a million ideas.

"As you can see we've used most of the original walls in here." Judith showed her around the large open space that served as both a shop and a little tea room. "My contractor worked so hard to make sure that all the artwork stayed. I'm thinking I'd like to use the mural as part of my business logo, but am not sure how to make it work."

"You could use the wheat as your logo with the initials of the shop incorporated within the design." Dusty took the sheet of tissue paper that the girl at the register handed her and the large marker. "See? Like this. It would be easy for you to get this same design printed on labels you can pick up at a local store and put them on the bags yourself. It will save you a fortune."

Dusty worked as she spoke, not really thinking of anything but to give the woman, a woman she'd come to admire, a helping hand. And if she gave her a little business down the road, it would be nice but not necessary. Dusty handed her the rough sketch as she looked around the shop.

"I love this." Judith turned when the little bell over the door chimed. The woman coming toward them looked like she was going to burst at any second. Dusty had never seen a woman look so enormous during her pregnancy. "Look at this, Kala. I have a designer and an advertising firm. And a bonus of a good friend. Kala, I'd like you to meet Dusty McGee. Dusty, this is Kala Trainer. She's married to Riss. "

Before Dusty could tell her no, she didn't have an advertising firm, Judith was pulling her along to a table and ordering tea and scones for them all. The woman, Kala, sat down and huffed at them. Judith laughed.

"You should have a couple. You are eating for a lot of you, you know." Dusty looked at Kala's belly, then at her face. She knew that she looked shocked but wasn't sure how to hide it from her. Judith continued talking before she said something really stupid. "I also have some jams for you to take back with you. I'll have Dennis load them up for you."

"I'm going to waddle over to the deli case too. I need something for dinner. I don't suppose you have any of those chicken breasts like you had marinated the other day?" Kala looked at Dusty when Judith moved off to check for her. "I'm sure you're slightly overwhelmed right now. Not that I blame you, but I get it. I understand you met a few protectors last night."

Dusty nodded and took a sip of her tea. She wanted to ask her if she was one too, when Kala laughed. Her head was starting to do that spinny thing again and she needed to get out. Dusty thought it was time she should go, and started to rise when Kala caught her hand.

"Don't. You're overwhelmed and out of sorts, but I can tell you that you're going to be fine. So will Kip." Dusty sat down but didn't put her things down just yet. "You can trust us. We are only here for your wellbeing."

It occurred to her at that moment that she'd been manipulated. Dusty wasn't sure when it had happened or why, but she'd been bamboozled into all of this. It hurt her more than she wanted to admit that she'd been so stupid to think someone wanted to be her friend.

"Judith didn't just happen to be in the store when I walked in, did she?" Dusty looked at the woman at the counter laughing with a customer. "I should have known that something was up. Why would a woman who has a place like this one need to go to the store — where there are enough chemicals in one box of cereal to supply a small country — instead of here? I'm so incredibly stupid sometimes."

"No, you're far from stupid. You're lonely is all. And you're right. A protector called us to help you with some of the questions you have running in your mind. And we were going to do it anyway, so decided today was as good as any. We protect those that mean something to us." Dusty looked at Kala when she spoke. "Your nephew, he's all right then?"

"I have no idea." Dusty fought hard with the tears but like usual, they won out. She stood up again, determined to leave this time. "He has shut me out as much as his mother ever did. And he blames me for everything.

Though I don't know why he wouldn't. I'm a major fuck up and I'm barely hanging on. I need to go. I have…I need to get home."

"Stay. Please. I want you…we want you to stay. You need a friend and we're going to be here for you." Kala patted the chair again. "Please sit down. We can help you if you let us."

"I don't know what I'm doing." As soon as the words left her mouth, Dusty knew it was true. "I'm failing him and I don't know what to do. He won't let me in. I don't mean just his room…he won't let me in his heart. He's closed it off to me. And so much of me wants to be in there, to be his friend, his aunt. But I don't know how to do that."

"He hit you."

Dusty put her hand over her mouth. The medic had told her she needed stitches, but she'd told him to just tape it shut…the wound, not her mouth. Though now that she thought about it, she should have had him tape that as well. What did she care if there was a scar or not?

"I'm sure he feels badly that he hurt you."

"And I'm equally sure he wishes he could have hurt me more. Though I don't know how he could have. He's already torn my heart out." Dusty sat down and watched as Judith made her way to them. Once she was seated, Dusty didn't look at the two women but told them what she was feeling. "I hate what I've done to him. I wish…I knew that taking him from his home was wrong, but I had no way of taking care of the money she owed in order for us to live there. And the place…I'm surprised that someone hasn't condemned that place. It was disgusting. The officer was really nice, but he said that the apartment and all its contents were seized by the state. They wouldn't even let me go in and get a fucking picture for him to take home of his poor dead mother."

"Have you told him what happened?" She shook her head at Judith. "He should know what you've given up for him. What you're doing for him. Then he needs a good kick in the ass for the way he's been treating you."

"I suppose Boss told you everything." When neither of them answered her Dusty looked at them. Judith looked guilty and Kala was looking at everything but her. When they still didn't answer, Dusty had finally had enough. "What is it you're trying really hard not to tell me? I think I can take it, and even if I can't I want to know."

"I can read your mind."

Dusty waited for the punch line, and when none was forthcoming she stood up. She was out to her car when she realized that she'd just lost a client, something she could not afford. As she brought her groceries into the house the phone was ringing. Answering it without checking the caller ID, she nearly dropped it when the man at the other end of the line starting talking.

"None of them will help you when it comes down to it. I've got him now because of my mark, and he'll turn to me long before he will you. He's mine and I plan to take him as soon as I can." The laughter made her think of nails scratching down a chalkboard, and she sat down on the floor as he continued. "I'm going to eat him alive…peel his skin from his tender body and then eat every part of him. Then when I'm finished, have eaten the last little morsel of him, I'm going to—"

The phone was taken from her and she stared at the man kneeling in front of her. She had no idea who he was or what he wanted from her. But before she could scream, if she could have, her vision blurred and she fainted.

~~~

Galin picked her up and carried her to the bedroom he'd seen her in earlier. She was light and he wondered briefly if she was eating any better than her nephew. Laying her down on the bed he reached for Michael. He appeared in the room in seconds.

"He's called her." Michael nodded and moved out of the room, only to return a few seconds later. He had a wet cloth in his hand, as well as a cup.

"I have brought her some tea. If you could wake her, she would do well to drink it. I think the sugar will do her some good." Galin was just reaching for it when Kip walked into the room. "I have had him come to your aid."

"Who are you? And what are you doing in my…?" Kip moved to the bed and took his aunt's hand. "What did you do to her? I'm calling the cops."

"I'm not the one that hurt her. The man from your dreams did it." Kip stood up and moved back from the bed, paling as he moved. "I'll not hurt you, either of you, but your aunt needs you to help me keep her safe. You too."

"I don't know what you're talking about. I just had a bad dream. My mom died and all, and I—"

Galin cut him off. "You dreamt about a man who changed into a large demon. And he grabbed your leg to bring you back to his hell with him. But something stopped him. I don't know if it was your aunt or the fact that you woke up. Whatever the reason, you're safe, for now." Kip was shaking his head and Galin went to him. Grabbing him by the shoulders, he shook him just a little. "Get a grip, boy. Your aunt has had a horrific scare and
~~~

she's fainted. What do you know about her that would help me?"

"Nothing." Galin knew that but he could see that it had startled the kid to say it aloud. "She took me from my home a month ago and has me staying here with her. As soon as I get enough money together I'm going back and staying in my home."

"It's gone." They both turned to Dusty, who was sitting up on the bed but not looking at them. "The Feds took it all. They went in and seized everything because your mom had been muling for someone and they rolled on her. The day she was killed they found over nine thousand pounds of drugs in her car, and she was stoned out of her mind."

"You lie." Galin knew that she wasn't and nearly told Kip that when he continued. "You'd say anything to make it so I didn't want to go back there. Well, I'm going and you can't fucking stop me."

"I'm not sure I want to anymore." Kip looked at him at his aunt's confession. "You might be better off living on the streets than here with me. I've done nothing to help you. I've given up…do you have any idea what a funeral costs? Thousands. And the hospital wouldn't even let me bury her without paying off her bills. All of them. I'm broke, Kip." She looked up then and Galin watched her face for any signs of hysteria.

"She had money. Lots of it when she went out of the house. I saw it." Galin watched Dusty as Kip spoke. "She said she'd be back and we'd go out to dinner. We were going to go to the park and spend the day. She and I were happy until you had to come in and take over. How do I know that you didn't have her killed so you could make my life terrible?"

"She was dead when I got there and you know it." Dusty stood up and moved toward the door. "I'm going to go outside. Say goodbye to your friend and then have him go. I'll…I'll see about making some arrangements for you to go to a home. You don't want to live here and I don't have the energy to fight you any longer. You win."

Galin looked at Kip when Dusty left the room. The kid was as close to crumbling as he'd ever seen a human to be. When he sat down on the floor, his back sliding down the wall as if he'd lost all feeling in his legs, Galin sat in the chair directly across from him.

"I don't know what to do now." Galin didn't either. "She really does hate me. I mean really hates me."

"I think you're wrong on that score, buddy." Galin stood up and put his hand out for the kid as he gave Kip some advice. "Here is what you should do…go out and let her tell you everything. I mean everything. Including how she feels about the crap you just said to her. And for the record, that was extremely mean of you. You're going to hate most of what she tells you, but you should know what she's been doing for you."

"You just want to fuck her." Before he could think about what he was doing, Galin slapped the kid on the face. Kip stared at him, shocked, and if looks were any indication, more shocked than Galin was at what he'd done.

"You say anything like that about her again, and I will hit you again. I've never…you're the rudest kid I've seen in a very long time." Galin looked around the room at the bareness of it before looking at Kip. "At first I didn't want to like her either. She didn't seem to be giving you what I thought you needed, and I even went so far as to have you clean up your room so that maybe she'd like you a little.

56

But you're a spoiled brat. Why should you be told to clean up after yourself? You're a teenager, not a baby. And look how much she has in comparison to what you have. Do you see any other room as well-stocked as yours is? Does she have a computer at this desk? Does she look like she's living in the lap of luxury? No. You want to know why? She's given it all to you. To try and make things better for you. I've never seen a kid have as much as you and not care a nickel for the person who has given up so much to give it to you."

"My mom was going to—"

"Your mom was going to take all that money she got running those drugs for her supplier and buy more drugs. And she might have taken you out to dinner, but you know what would have happened as well as I do. I didn't even know your mother and I'd bet she disappointed you more in one day than this woman has the entire time you've lived here."

Galin had been talking to Rose's protector when he'd heard Dusty whimper a few minutes ago. He'd run into the house so quickly he nearly didn't see her huddled on the floor with the phone still clutched in her hand. The look on her face...he knew that would give him nightmares for a very long time. "Your mother was a doper and a thief, Kip. The only reason she wasn't in jail when she was killed is because the police were hoping to catch her with her buyer."

"No. That's not right. You're—"

"Get out." They both turned to Dusty when she spoke. "I don't know who you are, but I want you out of our house. Now." Galin started to speak but she took a step toward him, and Riss was suddenly there pulling Kip to him and under his protection. As they all dropped to the floor, Galin heard the gun fire just as he covered Dusty with his wings.

~~~

It took over an hour to calm Kip down. He was screaming when Riss let him up, and didn't stop until Riss touched his fingers to his forehead. Now he just sat in the corner and looked out as if he was no longer in his body. But Dusty was who worried him the most.

"I should call the police." She'd said that five times in the last ten minutes and no one told her again that she'd called them. Twice. "I don't know what to tell my insurance company. I don't even know if this will be covered, do you?"

Galin didn't answer her but let her talk. Kala was on her way with Judith and they'd know what to do. Or he hoped they would. As she continued to pace the kitchen, Galin went to the stove and put on a pot of water. Tea, she needed tea. And to be honest, so did he.

He was busy pulling cups from her cabinet when he thought of her being beneath him. Galin had touched a human before, of course, but he'd never had one beneath him. His cock still ached and his body felt strung on a wire. He looked at Riss, thinking to ask him, but he was staring at him and Galin flushed.

"She is upset." Galin nodded and put a cup of the freshly brewed tea on the table and pulled her into a chair as Riss spoke again. "She has not asked what we are doing here or what happened that we needed to protect them from. I worry for her wellbeing."

"She'll be okay." He didn't know who he was trying to convince, him or Riss, but he sat with her when she stared at the cup. "Dusty, you have to drink this. It'll make you feel better."

"Someone tried to kill us." She looked up at him and he stared into the most beautiful blue eyes he'd ever seen. "I may be losing it, but I can hear you both just fine. And don't think I didn't see those wings, either. I did. I'm just trying my best not to freak the fuck out. I think I'm doing very well, too. This has been...I wonder what tomorrow will bring." The burst of laughter had him cringe. Dusty wasn't well, he could see that now.

She picked up the cup and took it slowly to her mouth. Her hand was shaking so badly that Galin thought she'd burn herself the way the tea was splashing everywhere. After taking a sip, she sat the cup into the saucer gently and looked at him. She asked him, very politely, who he was and what he was doing there.

"My name is Galin. I'm Kip's protector. You met Jacob last night." He'd been trying to reach the man since they realized they were all fine, but he'd not been there. They were coming up empty on locating him. "You're not going to freak out, please. I need you to remain calm so that I might explain everything to you. All right?"

"I need to have my head examined is what I need." She took another sip of tea. "If I ever have some goons shooting at me again and you brew some tea for me, there's a bottle of bourbon in the cabinet over the fridge, and I don't take sugar."

He nodded and smiled. "I will remember. Are you hurt? I've tried to check you several times but you slapped me away. I thought if you were truly hurt you'd either faint again or you'd pass out from blood loss. I can't see any blood but you could be hurt. I don't know a great deal about human women, but I know that loss of blood is dangerous."

"I'm fine. And no, I'm not bleeding, not from a gunshot wound anyway. My heart is hurting so badly, however, that I'm sure it bleeds all the time." She looked at Kip. "Did you put him into some sort of trance or something? He's scary quiet right now."

"It's called a veil, a sort of out-of-body sleep. Riss did it to help him calm. In a bit I'll have him take him out of it. He'll be better for the time to have his mind rest." Riss smiled at her when she looked over at him and Galin decided she was as calm as she was going to get. "This is Riss. He is a Mystic. You met his wife today, Kala. She is expecting his child. Agon, Judith's husband, will be here soon. He's putting a protection on your home that will keep you safe even when we are here with you."

"Should have done that sooner, I'm thinking. It might have saved me a ton of money." She got up, poured the tea in the sink, and pulled down the bottle of liquor. "I know that it's early but I just want a little."

She poured about two ounces into her cup before sitting back down at the table. He watched her, but she sipped it quietly and he knew that her mind was working out details. When she looked up at him, Galin felt his heart take an unexpected leap. She was more than beautiful, she was gorgeous. And the intellect in her eyes made him think that she was handling this a good deal better than anyone he knew might have.

"I want you to tell me what you know. I know you are aware of what's going on, and in order for me to protect Kip, I want you to tell me." Galin nodded, then shook his head. "Not very helpful there, buddy. You either tell me or I find someone who will."

"I don't know everything. Very little as a matter of fact. I know that Kip has been marked by a demi-god by the name of Markum and that he wants him. What he wants him for, I'm not entirely sure. But he will take him when he can. We're working on why Kip, but Boss seems to think it is because of his anger. Kip has a great deal of anger right now." She nodded and took another sip of the bourbon. "You spoke to him, Markum. He called you and spoke to you about Kip, I'm assuming. Can you tell me what he said?"

"I'm asking the questions right now. Maybe if you don't bullshit me too much, I'll tell you, but for now, I want answers." Galin found himself admiring the woman. She had spunk, he'd give her that. "This guy that wants Kip, do you think it's the same guy who shot up my house? And if so, why not use whatever hocus pocus he used to touch Kip instead of human guns and stuff?"

The both looked at Riss when he cleared his throat. "I do not believe it is the same person. This person who came here today wanted drug money that he feels is owed to him. In his mind your sister has given you money that was meant for him. He thinks...not very smart of him...but he believes that you're simply keeping money that he feels belongs to him. Markum has no use for either money or drugs. I believe it to be two separate entities."

Dusty smiled at him and Galin found himself wanting to reach for her. He curled his fingers under his leg to keep himself from doing what he wanted. She nodded toward Riss.

"Does he always talk like he's just come out of a novel? I mean, he could be an English teacher or something." Galin laughed when Riss snorted. "He even snorts all proper and English-like."

"Riss is my friend, but he is a little on the stiff side." Galin looked at Riss and smiled. "I've been telling him for decades that he needs to loosen up more, but the harder I try to make him talk like a human, the more he resists. I think he's destined to be proper and staid. But he is the kindest, most gentle man I know, and will protect you with his life if need be." Riss bowed before them both, bending at the waist and putting out his hand like in a Victorian novel as Dusty had said.

"Decades?" Galin kept an eye on her as she got up again and poured the rest of her drink into the sink. "I'm...what are you? I know you said protectors and Mystics, whatever that is, but truly, what the hell are you?"

"Protector of those that need me. A magical creature that will watch over, care for, and sometimes guide a person in the correct pathway." She nodded and he stood up slowly. "I've been assigned to watch over Kip for the rest of his life. I am his protector for all time."

"I have one too." Galin nodded and kept walking toward her as she stood there staring at him. "You're not going to...am I going to die? Soon? Is that why you're here?"

"No. Not that I'm aware of." She backed into the counter behind her and Galin took the last step to her. "I have a need to touch you. I don't know why this is happening but I want to touch your bare skin. To feel if it is as soft and silky as it looks. To taste it, to see if it tastes like the flowers in the spring."

"I think I'd like that too." He ran his fingers down her cheek and felt the heat of her skin as he touched her. Moving his fingers just a little lower, he touched her pounding pulse at her throat and leaned down to taste her there. As soon as his mouth touched her skin, Galin nipped hard at her throat and heard her moan. Lifting his head, he looked down at her. Her eyes were glazed, darker in color now. Her hot breaths fanned over his face as he watched her. When she licked her lips, running her moist tongue over them, Galin had an overwhelming urge to follow the same path and touch his to hers.

"I should very much like to kiss you." She nodded and tilted her head just a little. Galin lowered his mouth to hers and brushed it gently over her lips. As soon as he started to rise she ran her tongue over her lips again and he watched her moisten them. Galin lowered his head again and took her mouth.

He'd seen people kiss before. Couples leaving for the day would peck each other on the mouth or cheek and then turn to go. Galin had seen lovers kiss as well, passion running high as they devoured one another. But this was different; this was...this was delicious, amazing, and he wanted more.

*Galin?* He heard his name in his mind but wanted to ignore it in favor of the woman in his arms. *Galin, you are going to have to let her go. Kala and Judith are here.*

*I don't care.* He didn't either, and lifted Dusty up and sat her on the counter. *You go away too. I like this.*

*She is not yours to take.* Galin frowned at the second voice in his head. *Galin, let her go. She is not yours to take. You cannot have her now, she is...there is no way for you to claim this woman now.*

He looked down at Dusty when Boss told him to back away. It was the most difficult thing he'd ever done, but he did it. When he was five feet from her, Dusty looked at him, dazed, then jumped off the counter and walked up to him. The slap was less than he deserved, and he didn't try to stop her when she left the room.

"You are going to have to explain yourself." He nodded at Riss as he opened the door for his wife and Judith. "Not just to Boss either."

Galin knew that as well. He'd just broken one of the laws of his kind. But the problem as he saw it right now wasn't so much that he'd broken the law, but that he wanted to find her and break a few more. Instead, he lifted the veil off Kip and sat down with him. It was going to be a very long day.

# Chapter 4

Markum moved from the room and into the next without touching the floor. He enjoyed floating now that he had mastered it, and did it whenever he could. Even in his own cell. Just as he was ready to enter the hallway, someone stepped in front of him. He bowed before the man and stared at his bared feet.

"You smell of humans." Markum didn't even bother trying to deny it. He knew he did and loved the fact that someone had noticed. "I thought you were forbidden to go there until you were told you could. There will be hell to pay for this."

"I have found him." The being in front of him said nothing. Markum took that as a good sign and continued explaining. "The child that would help us in the other world. I have found him. He even bears my mark."

*Or he did*, Markum thought. Until someone had taken it from him. It was why he'd been to earth again today, trying to find the child before someone else did. But his mark that would call for him was no longer strong enough for him to summon the child.

"And this child you have found, what makes you think he is any different than the other dozen or so you have said was him? Have you a second sight, Markum? Do you possess a skill that none of the rest of us have?" Markum actually thought he had a great many skills that others didn't but said nothing. It had done him no good before, and he doubted that he'd be any more receptive this time. "I want to know what you think this child has that the others did not."

"He has an anger that boils from him. His hatred of people, all humans, is stronger than any I've come across before. And when I touched him, his leg, when he spoke with me, I could feel the connection immediately." Markum was jerked from his position and lifted two feet from the floor as the being held him with his hand at his throat. "I only marked him for you, my lord. So that he would be claimed by you."

"You dared to touch a human? A human child without permission?" He was tossed across the room. "You have violated our pact laws. You have taken what did not belong to us."

"His protector was gone. He wasn't with him when I found him." Which was true. Markum had imprisoned him days ago. Just after that upstart from the Mystic's had embarrassed him. "I have made sure that no other protector has taken him in. He is yours, as I have said."

"You lie." Markum started to stand but didn't need to when he was lifted up again. "You smell of...you have murdered a human, too?"

"I have." There was no point in denying it. He was sure that he smelled of the man that had dared to shoot holes into the home of his child. And for that matter, Markum wasn't sure why no one had asked him before. "He fought a good fight, but I am much his superior. Was much his superior."

"You fool." He was tossed away again, but this time leapt up before he could be touched again. As soon as the being tried to grab him, Markum lashed out with so much heat that he cut deeply into the fool. The second time he came for him, Markum hit him again, this time nearly severing his neck. Weak now, the being staggered toward him, but Markum had had enough. This time when he put up his hands in anger, he cut him in half and watched as he turned to dark ash. Markum was dancing around down the hall when he felt himself being summoned. Christ, he'd just killed an underlord, and one of good standing.

As soon as he entered the large chamber, Markum dropped to his knees. He wasn't stupid enough to think that he'd been called there to be congratulated. The being, the thing he'd just killed, worked for this man. And this man was one to be afraid of. As soon as he was only three feet from the man in the throne, crawling on his belly, he laid on the hot stone floor and spread his dark wings open.

"You have been busy, haven't you?" Markum cringed at the thunder in his voice but knew better than to answer without permission. "The being I sent for you has been murdered. Do you know what has happened? I'm feeling the loss of him just as if someone had killed him. Severed his bond with me without as much as a question to me as to my plans for him. You will answer me, Markum. I'm in no mood to fuck with one such as you."

"I have killed him, sire. Cut him with my magic, as I'm sure you are aware. But he accused me of things that were not true." Markum was told to sit up but he didn't stand. There was no permission given for that as yet. "He attacked me first, my lord, and when he did, it was all I could do to defend myself. He is dead because I'm a better man than him."

"You think so?" Markum nodded and the man laughed. "I don't believe you are much more than the shit beneath your own shoes, Markum. And I think if you thought about it hard enough you'd see I was right. You have murdered in my own world as well as the other. There are rules that must be upheld concerning the killing of others, even in our world. You will be required to pay for such deeds."

"Yes, my lord. I am aware of the laws. But I should let him kill me without defending myself?" The man said nothing and leaned back in his chair. Markum smiled. "I have found the child, sire. He is born."

"He is? Like the other times? Or is this one really it? As you have said to others countless times before, what makes this one so special?" Markum was startled out of his thoughts when his lordship spoke. "Yes, I know of your claims. This is what, the tenth, eleventh child you have found in the past decade? I grow tired of your findings. What of this one? You may answer."

"He has a fire like the ones that burn below us. His hatred is profound and he is without a protector." His lordship leaned forward and Markum forgot himself, so caught up in his attention. Standing up, he started to pace as he explained why this one was different. "This child not only has no protector, but the one that cares for him, another human, has the same anger burning in her. She is a woman who would die to protect the child, but it will matter little once I have convinced her to let me have him. And she will. She hates him as much as he does her. He is the one."

His feet were knocked from him as he made the turn to pace along the room. Markum nearly turned and attacked the person who would dare touch him when he realized who had hit him. His lordship was standing with a large blade in his hands, holding it at the ready. Markum dropped back down and spread out. He was going to die, he knew it. He'd gone too far this time.

"When in my presence you will not pretend you are on the same level as me. You are nothing." Markum seethed with anger as the man poked him in the back with the long blade over and over. When he stopped, Markum felt rather than saw the men come from behind him and lift him by his arms. His lordship opened his robe and freed his cock.

There were no words spoken as Markum took his cock into his mouth. It was thick and hot and Markum knew better than to turn away. He took each hard stroke down his throat as the man fucked him as hard as he could. When he came, spilling his seed on his face rather than down his throat, Markum cried out, knowing that he was being burned for his insolence. And the scar of it would be there for all to see, for them to know that he had angered this man.

"You will come here daily to let me mark you, Markum. And if I tire of you, there will be others that you will fuck for me." The guard that held him reached down and rubbed his cock to show Markum he would be the one he'd fuck. "I think…yes, I have decided to let one of them have you while I watch today. That way when you think you are better than me, you'll remember what will happen to you when you do."

His pants were ripped from him as the second guard held him bent over. As soon as his ass was filled, Markum cried out and had his mouth filled with the second guards cock. He was being fucked at both ends as his lordship watched. Pain was over him, his body seemed to be a festering pool of it. Yet they never stopped, only replacing one cock in his body for someone else's when that guard was spent.

A woman came from the shadows and moved in front of his lordship, took his cock into her mouth, and sucked him while Markum was being fucked. As soon as the man at his ass came, he grabbed Markum's cock from beneath and fisted him until he was hard as stone. The third or fourth guard—he'd long since lost count—came down his throat a few seconds later, not burning him but filling his belly with a vile nasty virus. As he laid there, filled with the poisonous cum, the man who had sentenced him pulled his cock free of the woman's mouth and spilled his seed on his chest and legs. Markum cried out with pain. He knew that before this punishment was over, he was going to be as ugly as the men who had held him down.

As he staggered his way back to his cell, he tried to think about what he'd do to each of the men who had violated him. It wasn't as if Markum had never had a man before, but he liked to choose his own partners and not to have them make him ill after. He vomited his belly clean of the poison and then entered his own shower to clean the rest off him. If that were even possible.

His body was an open sore, and it would be forever if he didn't find a way to redeem himself. The thought of having this done to him daily for all eternity made Markum want to go and find them all and kill them. But he couldn't and they knew it. His only hope was to find the child and bring him down here so that all could see what he'd already discovered. The child that would bring glory to them all had been born.

It was nearly dawn when he finally fell into a fitful sleep, the pain making it difficult for him to find even one comfortable position. But he dreamed of his redemption. Of the time when they would all bow before him. Markum just had to wait for the right time to make it so.

~~~

Dusty eyed the man as he sat quietly at her table. The rest of them were talking a mile a minute and shoving food at her every time they moved by her. She looked at Kip, who had not said a word since the two women had gotten there.

"You should try to eat something." She got up and pulled the case of candy bars she'd gotten for him today out of the cabinet. "I don't like that this is all you eat, but right now it's better than nothing."

Kip took one of the candy bars and held it in his hand. He looked like he was in shock, and Dusty found she didn't blame him. There was a shit ton of stuff being thrown at them both, and they still had their own shit to deal with. She looked at Galin and felt her face heat again.

She'd nearly let him take her on the counter. And the other man was there to see them do it. Every time she thought of his mouth on hers, she wanted to put her fingers over her lips to see if they felt as hot as they had when he'd kissed her. She looked at him again, and when he winked she felt her face heat more.

*You're very pretty when you do that. I have never seen a woman blush as much as you do. It makes me wonder what you would be doing had we made love on the counter.* Dusty looked at Kip and them back at the man when he laughed. *He cannot hear me. You can because I wish for you to. But no one else knows how much I would like to sit you on the counter again and taste the rest of your skin. Do you suppose all of you would taste that delicious? I wonder.*

*You should behave yourself. And no...I mean, I don't know if I taste that way. But you're not going to get to find out.* Dusty realized she was speaking to him the way he had her. *Why can I talk to you this way? I've never been able to do that before.*

*I would imagine it is because you are going to be my wife, and that is the way of things with our kind.* She looked at him, shaking her head. *I don't want it either and I'm trying to figure out how this came to pass. It was tricky of Him, I'll give Him that, but still.... And we might have to try something else if we're to get out of this without having sex. But I have to say, even kissing you brings all manner of thoughts to my mind. All of them have us both naked.*

*What do you mean, "He was tricky"? Who?* She looked in the direction he nodded and saw Boss, ignoring his comment about them being naked. She looked back to Galin. *You think He planned for you to take me on the...for you to kiss me like....*

*I believe when He told me I was to protect the boy it was to put me in your sights. I don't care for His tactics, but nothing more is going to come of it. Not if we're careful. I think we should work together until we have figured this out.*

*You keep saying that. Figure what out? Because I'm not going to marry you. Not for all the money in the world.* She felt his laughter and she wanted to hit him. *You listen here, buddy, right now I'm hard pressed not to get up and bash your head in. If I had to marry you, you'd not make it to the end of the day.*

*I'm immortal. You will be as well if we were ever to give in to our desires and have sex. But that isn't going to happen. At least I hope not. Actually, I do want it to happen, but not enough to wed you. I've no desire to have a wife.* Dusty felt her anger build up and it didn't help when he laughed again. *You are simply lovely when you are fired up.*

Standing up, she started toward him but he stood as well. She wasn't sure what he had been planning but she was leaving. Looking at Kip, she put out her hand. She wasn't sure he was going to take it, and when he did, the two of them moved toward the door. Agon, another arrogant man, stepped in front of her.

He stared at her for several seconds before he threw back his head and laughed. He moved out of her way and she stopped before leaving just to look at him. He bowed low and smiled at her when he stood up.

"I was going to ask you if you thought it safe to leave here, but I can see that whatever tried to take you on might be getting more than he bargained for. You are very…angry, are you not?" Not bothering to answer him, she went out of the house and to her car. Kip got into the passenger's side without her saying anything to him and she started the car. Dusty was glad she'd not had to remind him to buckle up. They were on the highway when he finally spoke.

"Those people have wings and they're in your house. I'm not…what do you suppose they want?" She glanced over at him and tried to think how to answer him when he spoke again. "The man in my dreams had wings, but his were dark, a bloody red dark, and he looked…hot."

"Hot?" He nodded and she looked out the window again. "I have no answer to that, Kip. I'm sorry. But he called me. Today when I got back from the store. He said he was going to…he said he was going to take you from me. And I'm pretty sure he's going to try, but I'm not going to let anyone take you from me."

Kip sat there through the next three lights without saying a word. When she pulled into a pizza place he turned to look at her. She felt her heart break for him. When he looked out the window again she wondered if he was going to speak and waited.

"Why not?" He looked at her when she didn't answer him. "Why aren't you going to give me to him? I don't blame you. I've not been very nice. I've been a real bastard to you. I know that now. I should have…Mom was never good with money. I don't have a clue why I suddenly expected her to have a stash for me."

"You have been a bastard to me, but I'm thinking…I should have been there for you. At least given you some clue as to what was going on with us." He nodded and she watched a tear roll down his cheek. "I'm not going to give you to anyone, Kip. You're my family and all I have in the world. I love you."

"But you could if you wanted to. No one would blame you, not even me." She reached for his chin and turned him to her. "I don't want to go with him. I don't know what he is, but I don't want to go. If you'll let me, I'll try harder to be a better kid for you. I don't want to be back in the same place I was before. Not in that kind of house, being without food or heat. I never…you've given me more in this one month than my mom did for me in all my life. I'm not even sure that she liked me all that much most of the time. I know she…she told me several times when she was high that she wished I'd never been born. I sort of forgot that in my being pissed off at you."

Dusty unbuckled her seat belt and slid to him. When she pulled him into her arms, he started sobbing and begging her to give him another chance. By the time he was finished crying she'd told him several thousand times that she loved him. When he leaned back on the seat he looked like he'd been drained, just as badly as she felt. Her tears, her cries had felt like they'd been wrenched from her as well.

They sat there for several minutes before Kip spoke. She didn't interrupt him. Dusty simply let him talk. She knew that they both needed this.

"She wasn't a good mom. Not even close. I think she loved me for the money when it was coming in but…it was mostly the checks she got every month for me that had her keeping me. And the food stamps." Dusty wanted to deny that but didn't know how. He was right by all accounts. "There were times when I'd have to steal food just to get a meal. I've never been to a movie or out to eat. Not unless you count the hospital food when she was…when she was hurt."

"I don't even count hospital food as food sometimes." He laughed, which was what she'd hoped for. "We should have a date night, you and I. A time when we go out and see a movie. I love movies. Especially when they're on the big screen. And dinner. I can't afford a great big meal, but a burger and some fries a few times a month should be fun, don't you think?"

Nodding, he sat there for several more minutes just staring out the window. Dusty knew that their relationship was tedious at best, but she was glad that he'd softened a little to her. When he turned to her she could see that whatever decision he'd come to was huge.

"The man who burned me, he's real, isn't he? I mean, I know that I had the burn and all, but he's real. It wasn't just a burn I got and then dreamed something else to cover it." She nodded, not wanting to lie to him again. "Will he kill me, you think? Or hurt me really bad?"

"I don't know. We'll have to talk to the people who do know." He nodded and looked out the window again. "You have a protector. Galin. He said he'd keep you safe."

"He didn't that night." Dusty nodded. "I'm thinking that if I'm going to be safe, I have to…we have to do it on our own. I don't think anybody is going to keep us as safe as we can. Not if we work together. Be…be a family."

"I think you're right." They got out of the car and walked into the high-rise where her business was instead of the pizza place. She was sure that whatever was in the break room would settle better than a pizza would about now. She showed him around and was glad for once that none of the staff was there. All five of them. For now anyway.

She'd heard from the landlord. Not only had he raised the rent to an outrageous amount, but he'd told her that she'd have to pay for the electric and the heat when it was on. Then there was the parking. The garage that they'd been told they could use was just behind the building she rented and they'd been using it for free. Now it would cost her if they stayed. She couldn't pass on that cost to her employees. She didn't pay them much as it was.

Denise had told her yesterday that she'd start looking for another building, but the amount they could afford wasn't going to make it easy. She had no deposit should they want one, no money for office equipment if it wasn't supplied, and if it didn't include some sort of break on the parking, she just couldn't do it. When Kip entered her office, he stood at the window that had a view of another building and smiled at her.

"You're not gonna get a tan from here, are you?" She smacked him gently on the arm as they both looked out. "You like working in an office? I would go crazy in here.

All cooped up with nothing but a desk. Unless you play games all day. Do you?"

"I do if you think about it. I play around with designs and templates." He made a face that made her think that he didn't agree with her assessment of games. "I love what I do. And I think I'm pretty good at it. I just hope I can keep doing it."

When he looked at her she told him never mind. They were having a good time right now and she didn't want to spoil it with news she knew might not happen. As they left the building she looked at her car and nearly stopped when she saw a man leaning against it. But then she recognized Galin and told Kip to go on ahead. She wasn't sure what to do with the man since he'd nearly had sex with her then told her he didn't want her.

"You should know that you were never alone." She nodded when Galin spoke. "I should like to have a conversation with you soon. We have things to work out."

"No, we don't. You're Kip's guardian and I'm okay with that. But there is nothing else we need to talk about. Stay away from me and we'll be just fine." He took a step toward her and she took one back. "You keep that up and you'll not be his guardian. I'm not shitting you, I'll go to your Boss and have Him give us someone else."

"Your protector is missing." She didn't know what that meant so said nothing to him. "Jacob hasn't been watching over you since the night after you were hurt. It was why you were injured the way that you were. I think that the man who hurt Kip took him."

"Are you saying I had something to do with that?" He shook his head and looked around. She had a feeling he was talking to whoever was watching over her now. "Carter said that you and Kip have made up. I'm glad for you both. But you must keep safe. There is much at stake for both of you."

"We're going to do that. On our own. We're not going to depend on anyone else." He started to speak but she cut him off. "I would very much like for you to watch over Kip but leave me alone. I don't want any more to do with you than you do me. Stay away or so help me, I'll go to someone that will make you—" He moved so quickly that she had no time to dodge him. He pulled her to his body just as fast, taking her mouth like he owned it.

The kiss was harsh, hard, and consuming. When he pushed his tongue past her lips and slid it along her own, she moaned and grabbed onto his arms. Then he gentled the kiss and pulled her tighter to his body, she could feel his erection and pressed her hips to his. It seemed that everything around them faded and it was just the two of them. When he lifted his head, Dusty had to hold onto him or fall, but when she looked into his eyes and saw the triumph there, she pulled back. When she nearly stumbled he reached for her, but she slapped him away.

"Is this a joke to you?" He started to speak again but she'd had enough. "I fucking hate you right now. The big bad immortal protector has to dominate the little human because he can. Does it make you feel good about yourself? Are you going to go back and tell all your friends how you made Dusty McGee pant for you before you tossed her away? Again? This is…stay the fuck away from me."

"I didn't mean—" She glared at him when he stepped in front of her. "You don't know what it's like for me. I don't want a wife, yet I can't think when you're around."

"Get over it." Getting into her car, she sat there for several seconds before she felt she could drive. Kip put his hand on hers when she started to put the car into gear. She looked over at him.

"Take a deep breath and don't kill us." She nodded and started to cry. Laying her head on the steering wheel, she cried and cried until, like she'd done for him, Kip pulled her into his arms and held her.

When she felt better she drove them home with extreme caution. As soon as they pulled into the driveway she went inside and ignored the people still there. Leaving them to do whatever they wanted, Dusty went to her room, stripped down in the bathroom, pulled her oversized tee-shirt over her head, and crawled into bed.

She hadn't gotten a damned thing done that she'd wanted to. The groceries hadn't been put away properly and not a bit of laundry had been done. Closing her eyes, she hoped that tomorrow would be better. But she was sure, as surely as she was laying there, that her life was no longer going to be even close to what could be considered normal.

# Chapter 5

Judith opened the door and slipped into the room that the lady at the desk, Denise, had told her was Dusty's. Well, she'd not really told her as much as she'd been thinking about her boss and Judith walked by her to see the other woman. Judith wanted to hire Dusty's firm, but she also wanted to find out if she was all right. Yesterday had been a hell of a day for the woman. The chair was facing the window and Judith started to leave, thinking that Dusty was out, when she started talking.

"You were right, Denise. I'm done. That call? It was the new landlords to tell me when the new rules start. My rent is increasing to fifty-five hundred a month, nearly twice what it is now, and we will no longer be able to park in the garage under the building or in front of this one at all. I suppose he thinks we should simply teleport ourselves to work. Unless, of course, we want to shell out an additional five thousand dollars a month per car. Then there is the added bonus of me having to sign a fifteen year contract that states if I should go out of business or move out of this building, I will be obligated to pay all and any money owed for the rest of the contract. Oh, and let's not forget the twenty-two percent increase on the rent yearly until the end of the contract." There was a very audible sigh. "I'm so fucked. And out of business as of now."

"Not necessarily." Dusty stood up and turned to her so quickly when Judith spoke that the chair started going round and round as she stared. "You should shut your mouth. It's not very professional."

Her mouth shut with a snap and Judith sat down in the chair across from the desk. It took her a few moments, but finally Dusty sat down as well. She was embarrassed, Judith knew, but she waited for her to get her shit together.

"You weren't supposed to hear that." Judith nodded. "I mean, I was ranting. I know that it sounded whiney but I was only ranting. And Denise is the best person I know to rant to. She listens, offers advice I usually ignore and…and you shouldn't have heard that."

"I understand. And it was a pretty good rant as far as I could hear. But I don't think it's the end of your business." Dusty got up and went to a small table that held a tea pot and several little tins of tea on it. As she stood there making up a tiny tray with cups and saucers, Judith looked around the room. It was busy work and Judith was all right with it. But the office, now this was not the office of a ranting woman.

It was nothing at all like her home. Uncluttered and everything in a nice cubby, yes, but that was about all. There were shelves that held books and nothing else, a table with four chairs that were pushed all the way in and perfectly cleaned of anything but three pens that were in a neat row. There was not one personal thing in the room. When Judith turned back to Dusty, she was handing her a cup, then sat down in the chair next to her.

"I'm not allowed to hang things on the walls here. Not that I probably would, but I thought it would be nice to show off some of the work I've done. The landlords, new and old, are in advertising, and I think for some reason they think of me as some sort of competition." She shrugged. "I really want to apologize for what you walked in on. But you were uninvited."

"So I was. But I would like to talk to you about helping me with my company. I need someone like you to make me shine." Judith took a sip of tea as she let Dusty take it in. She could see that she was excited, but there was a sadness there as well.

"I'm really sorry, but as you know, I can't do it. Not now. I can't afford the kind of rent they're asking me to pay, and I can't work from home. I won't do that to either of us. It's a place where I go to relax and be me. I won't be able to do that if I know that there is a project waiting for me in the other room." She stood up and moved to the business end of her desk. "I have to be out in thirty days. I'll do what I can to get you started on some things, but that's about all I can do. The men that I rent from, they're larger, have a much bigger budget, and will be around long after I'm finished."

"I don't want them, I want you. And I have a building that you can use." Dusty paused in writing something down on a sheet of paper. "It's not far from my business and it's empty as of right now. The work being done on it will be done in a few days, and I want you to rent it from me."

"I can't afford a deposit right now. Much less the startup costs of opening somewhere else. Everything that's in this office is a rental and not through me. Even the desks we use out there, we're renting from the landlords. It's all I could do to get started. And after a while…well, with Kip living with me, my finances have changed a bit."

"I completely understand. But as you have no idea what the building looks like, how much the rent is, or even what's already in the thing, you can't make a decision just yet." Judith stood up. "Come on. We'll have a look at it now."

Dusty was putting on her coat when Judith reached for Michael and Agon. Each of them answered her with a laugh. She loved these men and knew that if anyone could pull off what she wanted these two could.

*Is the building across from us still for sale?* Agon said it was. *I want you to buy it for us. And if you can see about moving some of the workers over there to make it look like they're renovating it, I'd appreciate it. I'm bringing Dusty over and she's thinking of renting it from us.*

*We do not own it, love. Do you think it possible I call the bank first?* Agon laughed again. *Or do we want to give her hope?*

*She needs hope so bad right now, it's going to be a slow uphill battle to bring her around.* She told him about the conversation she'd overheard. *I need her. I think that she's going to be married to Galin soon, if she doesn't murder him first, and I want her to be friends with me.*

*I will have it ready.* Michael asked her what else she would need when Agon told her he was calling the bank.

*What do you know of office equipment for a large advertising firm?* He told her nothing. *Then could you come to her business, look around, and try to make her think all that stuff is already there? I don't mean all of it, but like desks and lighting. You know, business stuff.*

*Of course. Business things. I shall see what I can do for you. Does this woman…you think that she and Galin will match well? I ask because I do not believe she is happy with him at the moment.*

*She's not.* He told her he didn't want her and has told her *that they'd have to work around it.* I think the next time I see *him, I might have to work around his head. The arrogant idiot.* Michael laughed and told her to be careful. *I will.*

By the time they'd made it to the street Judith had heard from Agon twice. The building was theirs and there were nine men working on it as they spoke. He had Dan go over to it immediately to tell them if it was a sound buy.

*The banker was most cooperative. He has had this building on his books for some years and was ready to have it taken down for the taxes. I have gotten a very good deal on it. One dollar.* She asked him how he'd done that. *We are to make improvements on it within eighteen months and have a renter in after two years. I assured him that would be no problem. While I was there, I purchased two more such buildings. You will soon have more friends than you know what to do with.*

And not only had Michael been able to see what they'd had in her other building, but he'd been able to purchase the things in the office for nearly nothing. *It was very used. Perhaps we can purchase more such items for future use. I do believe that was the most fun I've had in some time. I have never wiggled before.*

*Haggled. It's haggled, not wiggled.* She thanked him. *You've done very well, Michael.* I just hope we can convince *Dusty this is the right move for her.*

*You are doing well, my lady. I am very proud of you. Miss Dusty will not know what has hit her.* Judith hoped so. She really liked the girl.

~~~

There were half dressed men all over the place and each of them seemed to be having a wonderful time.

Dusty watched as one man, who was obviously in charge, moved up a ladder like it was as easy as walking on the ground. She noticed he had a mark on his arm and then saw that all the other workers did as well. She thought it was something of a carpenters mark, but Judith came up behind her and smiled.

"They're protectors too. When they have a charge, a person they've been watching over, die, they come and work here until their time is up for rest. Most of these people will be moving on in a few weeks. Others, like Dan, will stay forever. He needed it." Dusty watched as he pulled sheet after sheet of drywall down like they were nothing more than sheets of paper. When he turned and caught her staring at him, he winked and came toward her.

"Your building, I presume?" She shrugged, but Judith told him yes it was. "Good. It will be lovely when we have finished with it. There will be nine offices on this floor and three on the upper. Someone had used it at one time as an apartment, so it will be a nice office for you." He took her upstairs and she could see it all from his description.

"What about those windows…do you know what they look out over?" Dan took her to the boarded up window and stood behind her. When he touched his hands to her head just above her ears he told her to close her eyes.

There it was, the view. And what a view it was. She could see a park with a swing set and two strollers sitting near a park bench, while the women watching over them, each with one hand on a handle, spoke as friends would, friendly and with laughter. Trees in the park danced in the wind that was blowing gently. Cars moved along a road that looked like a residential area, and there was a large pond just a little further out from the park. She turned to look at him when he took his hands away.

"You would like this view, I take it." She nodded. "I could enlarge the opening for you. Make the window twice the size it is now and put it from floor to ceiling." She started to nod, then shook her head. "You wish it to be bigger?"

"It's not my building. I mean, I'm thinking of renting it from Judith, but I don't have it and it's only going to be a rental if I do. You should really check with her about any changes like that. I'm thinking that none of that will be cheap. She might want no window at all." He smiled at her and she had a feeling he was humoring her. "I'm not going to be saddled with a bill that I can't afford because you think you can bamboozle me into something she doesn't want."

"Bamboozle? I have not heard that word in centuries." He laughed heartily and she smiled at him. "I would never harm you in any way, my lady, but would very much like to have you pleased when you sit in a building that I have given care to. If Lady Judith does not disagree with your window, I shall have it put in for you. But I do not believe she will care."

Dusty wasn't so sure…windows were expensive. She knew because last year she'd had all new ones put into her home, and she was still making payments on that. Then there were the ones she'd had to replace when that guy had shot up her home. Dusty just realized she'd never gotten a bill for that. Making a mental note to call the people, she moved around the large room thinking of all the things she could do with it. If she rented it. And boy oh boy, did she want this office building.

It was perfect for her...lighting all over the place, electrical plugs every couple of feet. The break room was empty, but she had an old table at the other building that belonged to her. Several of the desks were oak, one was cherry. Their smooth surfaces had her itching to run her hands over them just to be sure.

As she was shown around the rest of the building she fell more and more in love with it. The desk that had been left behind by the former tenants would also be saved, and was in the perfect place for her office, looking out over the room but with the view of a lifetime behind her. Dan thought it to have been put in the building, then walls built around it, it was so large.

By the time she was ready to beg them to let her rent the building, Judith had invited her to lunch at her shop to talk. They were sitting down to a crisp salad with fresh vegetables and grilled chicken when Kala walked in. Dusty was so excited about the building she didn't even think it odd that these women always seemed to be together. When her tea was brought to her, Judith told her the rent.

"That's not enough." Judith cocked a brow at her and Dusty blushed. "I'm sorry, but you know that it's not. I mean, I'm paying more than that now."

"You are, I'm sure. But we have gotten a grand deal from the city. And part of the deal was to have a renter by the time we are ready to open the doors. The rent will be four hundred per month and that's final. Or you can find another place to work." Dusty looked at the building and knew for as much as she didn't have much in the way of choices, the building was perfect for her. "You can start moving in tomorrow. Kala and I already have enough business for you to keep working for a long time."

"It's a big step." Judith nodded. "I want it very badly. And it will be perfect for Kip too. He can walk here after school instead of taking a long bus ride to the house."

"I'll have the contracts drawn up in the morning, and in the meantime, you and I are going to talk business. Then you and Kala. She and I are working on three projects right now. My dad's house is being opened as a halfway house in a few weeks to help kids get on the right track. We have a small company that provides men and women who have been out of the work force for a while help with getting the right look and the right letters to land a job, and there is my PP&J."

She was officially overwhelmed. When Kip got home from school he sat in the kitchen with her and listened to her rant then rave about the building and what was going on. When she put a plate of food in front of him, he looked at it for a long time before he looked at her.

"You don't cook." She nodded and sat down with him, looking at her own plate. "Nah, you don't cook. You put stuff together but you don't cook."

"I hate it actually." He grinned. "I suppose you love to cook. If you say yes, I'm going to hire you to cook for us. I don't even care if it's edible."

"It will be, I promise. When there was food, I'd make whatever I wanted and I got to be pretty good at it." She shoved her plate away after she took a bite…it wasn't fit to eat. "How about tonight we have a sandwich, and tomorrow night, I fix dinner? For the two of us."

"I have a better idea. We order pizza and pig out on it tonight and forget there is a tomorrow." Kip laughed and told her it was a plan. "Good, and you'll do your homework while we wait. I don't know a great deal about sixth grade, but if you need my help…well, we can look it up."

After dinner Kip had gone to his room but left the door open. She was sitting at the table and making notes on some of the things she wanted to work on with Judith's business when Galin sat down. She tried her best to ignore him, but he was just too…everything…for her to make that work. When he lifted her chin up she looked into his eyes.

"I've been very rude to you." She nodded and he laughed. "I had hoped you'd say that I wasn't that bad, but you are more honest than I am."

"I kinda doubt that. You seem to not be able to tell a lie." He told her that was true. "Good, then answer this for me. What makes you not want a wife? Not that I want you as my husband, but why are you so against having a wife?"

A cup of tea appeared in front of her and she tried not to be startled by it. Taking a sip, she knew immediately that it was a brew that he had made. She had no idea why she thought that, but she loved it and waited while he took a sip of his own cup.

"I have been on this earth for more decades, more millennia, than most protectors. And in all that time I never saw a single marriage or partnership that was perfect." She stared at him as he continued. "I wondered most times why the couple ever got together, ever even saw something in the other to have said they'd spend their entire lives together. So I thought that if I never married — which I think is an excellent idea — then I'd never have to be disappointed in someone that I'd be spending the rest of my life with. And with a person like me, it would be a very long time. Can you imagine how much hatred there would be after a time? How many arguments that we'd have? And the—"

"Oh yes, I can see how many arguments one would have being married to you. Even being in the same room with you causes me to want to get up and knock you on your ass." She stood up and so did he. "You dimwitted moron. How can you be in the position you are in thinking the way that you do? No, you do not get to answer that. Whatever spilled from your mouth right now would make me go out and buy a gun just to shoot you with. Of all the...you cannot believe that drivel you just spat out. People were born to argue. I love a good argument."

"I can see that you do. But it's not something I want to do with the woman I'm supposed to love." Dusty stared at him for a few more minutes before she went to Kip's door. "What are you doing? He needs to rest."

"Get in there and never come out when I'm in the house. In fact, I think you should make it so that I never even have to see you again. If I do then I don't know what I'd do to you." He came toward her and she had a feeling he was going to touch her, and she glared hard at him. "You touch me right now and I will bite your hand off then beat you with it."

She was never any good at snappy comebacks and was sure he was going to laugh at her. He stood there staring at her for several seconds before he went into the room. But before she could close the door, he came back and pulled her body to his. This kiss was different from the one before, and she knew he was going to take her.

Her body pressed against the wall and she clung to him. There was no doubt that he wanted her; his thick cock was at her pussy and he was rocking into her like he was actually making love to her. When he cupped her breast, thumbing her nipple until she cried out quietly, she nipped at his neck when he leaned down to bite her through her blouse and bra.

"I want to take you right here." She nodded at his statement and thought about telling him to do it. But he lifted her up higher on the wall and licked a path from her bra to her navel and rolled his tongue around the sensitive area. When he lowered her down the wall he took nips and bites of her skin until she wanted to beg him to take her then.

She had no idea how they made it to her bedroom. Suddenly the bed was beneath her and he was pulling at her clothing. As soon as a cool breeze blew over her nipple, Galin was taking it into his mouth as he pulled at her pants. She curled her fingers into his hair as he suckled at her breast.

There were no words spoken between them as he moved down her body. She was wet and ready for him, and when he nipped at her hip, she tried to pull him back to her mouth. But he was determined, and when she felt his tongue roll lazily over her belly button again, she sobbed at him to take her.

She came when he opened her nether lips and suckled at her clit. She came again when he slid his fingers into her. Dusty rode his mouth, knowing that she was going to scream when she came this time, and reached for the pillow near her head to cover her mouth. When he bit down on her, bringing her to a climax that made her eyes roll to the back of her head, Dusty knew that he was going to fuck her. And she could not wait.

"I should like to come on you, spill my seed on you and watch you peak again." He fisted his cock and her mouth watered at the length and thickness of him as he leaked pre-cum onto her. "When I enter you, I will not be able to hold on. I have wanted to release in you for days now."

"Please." He nodded and moved along her body as he held his cock. When he was at her entrance, she felt him fill her slowly and she rolled her hips up to have him take her. As soon as he breached her maidenhead, she screamed out his name and he stopped moving.

"You were a virgin?" She nodded, knowing that if he moved now she'd come again even though the pain was incredible. "I'm sorry. I had no idea that you—"

Dusty rolled her hips when he did. He was moving in and out of her slowly and she knew that he was trying not to hurt her again. Wrapping her ankles around his hips she pulled his mouth to hers and kissed him. When he lifted his head, he wiped at the tears on her cheeks with his thumb.

"You are wonderfully tight around me." He moved her hands to the top of her bed and wrapped her fingers around the headboard. "I have thought of you this way. Tied to this bed as I explored you. I don't know why that appeals to me, but it's all I have thought of."

"Are you into bondage?" He pulled at her nipple hard and she moaned at the pain and pleasure. "I'm not sure how I feel about that. I wouldn't mind trying it with you. I need to come again…will you give it to me?"

"I would like that very much as well. I don't want to hurt you, but I need to be overpowering to you. I should very much like to paddle you as well." She nodded and moaned when he pounded into her harder now. "My cock aches to fill you, my balls are tight against my body, and all I can think about is seeing you bent over my lap while I spank you."

She rolled him over and sat atop him. Dusty felt his cock like it was hitting the back of her throat and moved over him slowly. He sat up and pulled at her nipples until she cried out, then he bit down on one then the other until she thought she'd die from it.

"Release for me, Dusty. I want to feel you when you do, see your face when you have your pleasure." She bowed back and cried out when she came. He held her tightly against him as he suckled her breast. When she was coming down, her body nearly lax over his, he rolled her to her back and took her hard.

Her climax took her breath away. She cried out his name over and over as he slammed hard inside of her. Just when she was ready to beg him to stop, her body spent, he threw back his head and roared. She felt his hot cum touch her as he filled her. Dusty held on to him as her own body released again and again. When he dropped over her, she felt him roll, taking her with him until she was laying over him, sated. Closing her eyes, she let sleep take her.

# Chapter 6

Galin moved about the house, keeping an eye on the windows and doors as he moved. He'd just left Dusty's bed and he felt…well, he'd never felt this way before, and wasn't sure what to call the feelings. Kip was with the night watcher and he decided that he'd let him go and sit with the boy for a while. But Boss standing in the living room startled him.

"You have taken her." Galin nodded. He couldn't lie to Boss and found no reason to do so. "Will you marry her now?"

"No." Boss only nodded and Galin had a moment of fear. But all He did was turn and walk out of the house by simply fading through the wall. Galin started to follow but found himself in Tholan's office instead.

"You have been sent to me." Galin sat in the chair where his friend and boss indicated. "I have a list of things you are to do from now on. I…you have messed up severely, Galin. He is most upset with you."

"I'm not going to marry her. I know that was His plan when He put me to watch over Kip. But I don't want a wife, nor do I feel that I should be forced into it. So if that's what the rules are, then you can just tell Him I refuse." Tholan shook his head and Galin felt his body tense. "What is it I have to do, Tholan?"

"If you wish, you may continue to watch over Kipling. But you are no longer to have any contact with the woman. She will no longer be able to see you or hear you, no matter what. Her watcher will not give you —"

"No." Tholan raised a brow at him in question. "No. I won't not see her. That's not fair to either of us."

"Be that as it may, it is what He has said." Tholan picked up the paper and looked at him before reading. "You will do as he says, Galin, and not be punished more. He told me that you have no wish for a bride, and it is completely unfair of you to make her suffer when you are only wanting to bed her. You are lucky this is all He has decreed for you."

He got up to pace. Galin was trying to think what was going on, and all he could think was he was being blackmailed into something that he didn't want...had never wanted. This wasn't fair, and he wanted to hunt Boss down and tell him that. Before he could leave to go and do just that, Michael came into the room.

"You will do as you are told." The thunder in his voice made Galin drop to his knees and his wings to open. Anger was not something he'd expected from Michael, but he was upset too. They were ganging up on him and Galin wanted to fight back.

"I cannot be in the same house with her and not talk to her. We have slept together. Had sex. What will she think when I don't come to her if she calls?" Michael said nothing and Galin looked at him. "Is this a plan to make me do what you want? Is this how you'll make me marry her?"

"Nay, it is not. Do you wish to stay with Kipling or not?" Galin had to think about that for several seconds before nodding his head. "Then you will do as you are told or so help me, you will not like the consequences. Understand me?"

"I do." Galin stood up. "But you will also understand that if anything happens to her because I cannot help her, then I will quit you all."

Galin left the rooms and made his way to Kip. The other watcher was still there, and as much as Galin wanted him gone, he knew that the other protector would be in a better frame of mind to keep Kip safe right now than he'd be able to. His mind was a turmoil of confusion. Making his way to the bedroom that Dusty slept in, he watched her sleep until the sun rose in the sky. When she opened her eyes, Galin felt his heart twist in his chest and he knew he'd made the right decision. There was no way he'd spend all his life with the same person and be happy. And for as much as she loved a good argument, as she'd told him, he wanted peace. When it was time, Galin made his way back to his charge's room.

Kip moved around the room as if he'd not slept well and would like nothing better than to crawl back into the bed. Galin tried to keep him focused on his tasks, but his own mind was adrift so he had a hard time as well. When Kip was sitting at the table with a bowl of cereal in front of him, Dusty came in. Galin wanted to pull her into his arms and tell her everything would be all right.

"I have two meetings today. I should be home in time for dinner." Kip nodded and Galin told him to speak to his aunt, not nod. The boy perked up a little but still looked exhausted.

"I'll make us some dinner, if that's okay?" Dusty nodded and sat down with him. When she winced a little, Galin smiled. He'd done that to her. She looked around the room and he wondered if she was looking for him.

"Have you seen Galin today?" Kip shook his head. "Me either. I wonder where he might be. He's still your guardian, I guess, but…well, he'll be around I'm sure."

"I guess he's supposed to be with me all the time. Maybe when he's working with me, you aren't supposed to see him." Dusty nodded but still seemed distracted. "You like him, don't you?"

"I don't know. It's very complicated. And he has these ideas that are…irritating." She got up and walked to the sink to dump her untouched tea before she continued. "I was wondering if you could give him a message for me if you see him. Tell him…tell him I said thanks."

"Thanks?" She nodded at Kip and he shrugged. "Okay, if that's what you want. I don't know if I'll see him or not, but I'll tell him. Are you okay?"

"Yes. I'm very okay. You?" Kip shrugged, and before Galin could tell him to answer her again, the boy stood up and kissed his aunt on the cheek before going back to his room. Instead of doing what he wanted, like pulling Dusty into his arms and kissing her as well, he made his way into Kip's room.

Galin went to the grade school with Kip for the rest of the day. He was bored most of the time, but during lunch he got to talk to a couple of other watchers that had children that sat with Kip. While they were talking about nothing really, one of them brought up Markum.

"I heard that he is near us all the time now. That he's waiting to take our charges when we least expect it. And that someone from the training area had told him to go

Galin

away. Is that true?" Before Galin could tell them that it was true about the training area, one of the others spoke up.

"I heard that there was a sword fight and that many men were involved." Galin rolled his eyes. "And that two of the others were injured."

"There was no fight. He was told to leave and he did." They all turned to look at him. "I was there as well. He was told to leave and he did so. I doubt we've heard the last of him, so we'll be prepared for him at all costs. He is an evil man and will stop at nothing to get what he wants."

The conversation moved on and Galin found himself thinking about Dusty, wondering what she was doing and how she was feeling. He flushed slightly when he thought about the things he'd confessed to her last night, and wondered how she would feel if he were to tie her to the bed and have his way with her. Then he thought of what his punishment was.

Never to speak to her again. That was harsh, but he could see why. It would hurt her more and more to have him around her and him not marrying her. And a woman who had saved herself for all these years would want marriage. He watched Kip move through another class as Galin thought more of his aunt.

She was not like other women he'd taken care of in the past. Not that he'd ever slept with any of them, but he had known them by watching them daily. Dusty had been through so much and had seen a great deal as well. But she had taken her nephew in as her own without any help, or for that matter knowledge, of how to raise someone. As far as he could tell, she was doing a splendid job of it as well. Kip was going to be a good man when he grew up.

"I know you're there." He looked at Kip when he spoke. "I know you're listening to me but for some reason not showing yourself. So this is good. I wanted to talk to you about something. And if you can't tell me how stupid I am, then that's good too."

They were walking home from class and Kip has stopped at the PP&J to pick up a few things his aunt had asked him to. They were going to have grilled chicken and salad for dinner.

"You told me once that the man who hurt my leg was trying to get me. I think I know why. It's because I was so mean to my aunt, right? I brought him here because I was a real bastard."

Galin leaned closer to him and answered him. *It's nothing to do with how you and your aunt came to know each other, and everything to do with this person being evil. You are a good young man.*

"Good young man. I like the way that sounds." He walked another block before he spoke again. "I'm not though. Not a good young man. There were times when I had to steal stuff to have something to eat. I lied to the landlord a lot. Especially when my mom was either stoned or not there. Hadn't been there for days, as a matter of fact."

*You did what you needed to survive.* Kip nodded as he moved up on the porch and into the house. *You cannot take on the blame of things you had no control over, Kip. Had you not done what you did, then you'd not be here now. That would be a great loss to us all.*

He watched Kip cut up the chicken then put it into the oven after he finished dipping it into batter. Then he cleaned up his area, scrubbing down not just the cutting board but the knife, counter, and his hands. As he moved to bring things from the refrigerator to the counter to make a salad, Galin thought of the file that he'd seen on the boy.

*Do you know that most of the time — and I do mean most of the time — others in your situation would have given up? But you didn't. You made it work for you and your mother. Because without you, she might have died long before the day you did lose her.* Kip paused in his cutting of a carrot and Galin felt badly for bringing her up. *She was a good woman in her own way. She did keep you safe a few times.*

"I was seven when she stopped that druggy from taking me. He was going to hold me until she gave him the drugs she couldn't pay for." Kip snorted. "I shouldn't have been in that situation in the first place, but she didn't let him take me. Pounded him in the head with that ball bat that sat by the door until he dropped me and ran off."

*See?* Kip nodded and cut up his carrot as well as a cucumber. *She did love you very much.*

"And I loved her." Galin watched the boy cook and marveled at his ease at the task. He had a salad finished in no time and was putting rice on the stove to cook by the time he sat down to finish his homework. When the phone rang he answered it with politeness and a smile. But it soon turned to fear as he listened to the caller. Galin moved close to the boy, knowing without a doubt who was on the other end of the call.

"I don't know what you want, but you'd better stop calling here. My aunt won't like those things you're saying to me." Galin told him to hang up the phone and was relieved when Kip finally did. But he was shaken and afraid, and Galin told him to call the police.

"I should call the police." He even picked up the phone, but put it back as he sat back at the table. Try as he might, Galin couldn't make him call. It was nearly an hour later when his aunt came in.

She'd had good day, he could tell. Even Kip remarked on how happy she looked. Galin told him to tell her about the call but Kip ignored him. By the time his night watcher came to the house, Galin was as frustrated as he could be.

"He did not want to ruin her mood." Galin looked at Michael when he appeared in the kitchen with him. "Kipling decided that having her smile was better than worrying her, I believe. And in his own way, he was right. She has had few days where she has been as carefree as she was this evening."

"But he's afraid. What if that was Markum and he threatened him to —?"

Michael cut him off and Galin sat down hard in the chair. "It was him. He called to tell him that he was coming back for a second round of torture. I don't know all the details of the conversation, but he did frighten the young man. Markum believes that he will get to the woman through the boy. It will be most unpleasant for them both should that happen." Michael sat down as well. "How was your day? I have always liked going to school with my charges. They are —"

"Why does he want Dusty? And what does he think we're going to do? Give her over to him?" Michael said nothing and Galin knew it was a part of his punishment for not marrying her. "You think to blackmail me with information about Markum? This is not becoming of you, Michael. To cause harm to someone just to make me do what you want."

Michael sat there for several seconds just staring at him. Galin started to shift uncomfortably on the chair before Michael finally spoke. And when he did, Galin knew that he'd hurt the man a great deal.

"I do not have to resort to harming another being to get what I want. I think it a bad idea anyway to leave you here so that you can see her. She will move on eventually and will have a happy life for a time. You will only make it harder on her until you and Kip leave this house. And you will should this thing with Markum pass. But you will leave her alone. She cannot have a life at all if you are a constant reminder of what she could have had." Galin started to tell him he was sorry but didn't get the chance. "I will speak to Boss in the morning to have you removed. It is becoming too much for you to stay here and not cause her trouble."

"Please don't do that, I beg of you. I'm not going to cause her any trouble. I just want to make sure she's all right." Michael said nothing. "Please, I beg of you. Don't take me from Kip or her. I want to watch over him. I need to protect them both. I love the young man...I think I have loved him from the first. But to not see him, keep him safe...I won't be much good to anyone if I am constantly worrying for him."

"She will not benefit from your interference, Galin. The woman has been through enough without you causing her more heartache." Galin nodded but said nothing. All he could think about was how his heart was beginning to ache as well. "I will see what it is that I can tell you concerning Markum. But as far as Dusty is concerned, you are to keep your distance from her. Even talking to Kip about her, sending messages back and forth like school children, will not help her. Will not help either of you."

After Michael left with the promise that he'd be back, Galin sat in the darkened kitchen and thought about the rest of his stay with Kip. The boy and he were going to leave this house someday, and he could hardly stand the thought. The longer he sat there the more...he supposed the term would have been depressed...he became. He was depressed about spending his next few decades without her.

~~~

Dusty tried her best not to think of Galin and the fact that he'd just left her like he had. She thought she'd been doing a great job of it to only remember the night about sixty times an hour instead of all the time. He had left and that thought kept rolling around in her head. He'd left her. And he'd not been back once to see...well, to do anything.

She knew that her being a virgin would be disappointing to him. She had no experience in what to do to please him, and even though he'd come, she knew that having a climax was not always that satisfying. She had been satisfied, of course, but she was sure he was slightly bored with her. Dusty turned when someone knocked on the door to her office. She smiled at Dan when he spoke.

"I see you're all moved in downstairs. If you don't mind me saying so, it looks better than I thought it would. Being a place where you use colored pencils and such. Your staff seems to be pleased as well." They were too, and seemed to love the new digs. "I have a few more things to finish up in this area, then you're on your own." He moved to the wall where large bulletin boards had been installed, with wipe off ones as well.

"You did an amazing job. I love it. And I think that the staff would have your baby too if you'd only look their way." He laughed. "But seriously, thank you. And I wanted to thank you for having your men help me move as well. I don't know what I would have done once they told me I was finished there."

She'd gone to pick up the last of her things from the old building when the new landlords, two men really, had met her at the door. They had told her that they were taking everything for cleaning fees, meaning, like she had thought, there would be no deposit coming her way. They had also called the rental company and had those items removed as well, so that all of her files and papers were strewn all over the floors. They'd not even put them in any kind of order, just dumped the drawers out and walked over them when they needed to get around.

She was trying to reason with them when Dan had shown up with about a dozen men and women. In less than an hour they had her things boxed up, the mess cleaned up, and a check in her hand for the deposit she'd had to put down when she'd opened for business five years ago. She didn't ask how he'd managed that, but was grateful for the extra money. It had gone a long way to filling out her otherwise empty checking account.

"They had no right to do what they had done, and we simply showed them the error of their ways." She laughed when he did. "I did nothing that most wouldn't do for you had they been there. You're a wonderful human, and Kala and Judith have done nothing but speak your praises since they have met you."

She doubted it. In her experience most people would move on rather than get involved. Dan helped her move the desk where she wanted it, then he helped her hang a display of one of the large advertising campaigns she'd worked on, as well as several smaller ones she was just as proud of. She looked around the room, smiling.

"You look good here." She nodded and hugged him to her. He held her for a few seconds longer then looked down at her. "I need to tell you something."

She backed from him, thinking that something had happened to Kip, and reached for her jacket to go to him. But Dan put his hand on her arm and she stilled. Whatever he had to tell her couldn't be good, but she had a feeling it had little to do with her nephew.

"He is fine." She nodded and sat when he asked her to. "The man, Markum. Have you been told much about him?"

"Only that he's trouble and that he hurt Kip. I know that the protectors are watching us very closely and that everyone is on alert. Do you know more than that?" He nodded and she leaned back in her chair, suddenly more afraid than ever before. "Are you going to tell me that Kip is going to be hurt by him?"

"You both will be. But you will die if you are not careful." She nodded and felt her mind seem to freeze up. He was on his knees in front of her when she realized she'd zoned out for a few seconds. "I need for you to take extra precautions as much as you can. He is not a very nice...he is evil, and will do evil things to you if or when he captures you. Do you understand what I'm telling you?"

"And what do you suppose I should do, Dan? In the event you didn't notice, I don't really have a great many skills to fight against someone evil like him." Dan put out his hand, and in in the middle of his large palm was a medallion with a long gold chain. "What is that?"

"It's magical. And it will protect you like nothing else can. You must wear it at all times and never remove it. Kip has one as well, and he too has been warned about taking it off. It will give you extra strength to care for the both of you should he take you." She didn't touch it, but stared at it before speaking again.

"Galin has a mark like this on his right shoulder. And so do all of you, right?" Dan nodded but said nothing more. "Is he all right? Galin, I mean, is he all right? He sort of disappeared from my life and I feel...I'm sort of lost without him."

"He is well. Because he has lain with you, he is being punished by being kept from you." Dusty had a feeling that Dan shouldn't have told her this, but he smiled at her. "You'll be able to speak to him should you want to, but it will seem silly when you cannot see him. Trust me when I tell you, he is near you all the time when Kip is close at hand."

"He's still watching over Kip?" Dan nodded again and stood up behind her. He was putting the chain around her neck when she thought of something else. "I was wondering about if I were to have a baby by him. We didn't use...we just...there was no protection when we had sex."

"Sadly there will be no child from this union." She nodded and felt a bit depressed by it. "You will keep this on? You'll keep watching even though you are being protected by the others? The wolf and the panther that you have working for you, I have warned them as well to keep an extra eye out for you. They will know before you that someone with ill intent is around."

That had been something she'd known in the back of her mind, but neither of them had told her. Then a few days ago, both Dale and Paul had come in her office and confessed, she supposed would be a good term for it, that they weren't human and they would keep an eye on her.

"I will." He sat in front of her. She looked at him and felt tears threaten before she spoke again. "I thought that I'd bored him or something."

"You did not." Nodding, she got up to put the rest of the things she'd brought from home on her desk. "There are some supplies that we're to bring to you. I found them in the other building when we were working there. Things that you can use. Judith is making me a list of things that she wishes for you to have as well."

Dusty turned to look at him, glad for the sudden change of subject. "You found them, or you went and found them?" When he didn't answer her she turned back to what she was doing. "I'm beginning to think that I've been bamboozled into this building and job for Judith. Am I right?"

Dan laughed. "She does have a way of getting what she wants." He stood up when several men walked in loaded down with boxes. "She has wasted no time in getting you settled in with things she thought you'd need."

They put the things in the room next to her office, which was going to serve as a supply cabinet for the entire building. She was just locking the door, making a mental note to tell Denise that they were in there, when she turned to Dan. He looked like he knew what she was going to say and smiled at her. She took a deep breath to tell him what was on her mind.

"Don't gloss over the truth to me again. If you know something or hear something, or even just have stuff for me, just tell me. I want you to be my friend." He nodded. "Can you please thank Judith for me?"

"I shall, but I think you'll get to do that yourself. She is coming down the hall now. With Kala."

They both turned when the two women walked in. Kala was told to sit down and she did so without argument. The poor woman looked ready to fall over, exhausted.

"You are going to go to dinner with us. I've already had someone go to the school and pick up Kip. He's such a wonderful young man. I might adopt him myself." Judith sat down. "And before you get your panties in a twisted knot, you should know that Riss and Agon are going too, so you won't feel ganged up on."

"I think she can hold her own with you." They all looked at Kala. "You're pushy and bossy, but I think that Dusty is going to stand up when she needs to most and knock you on your fine ass. Me, however, I am going to just sit here and be ginormous and wish that I could have my babies now instead of in four months."

"You have four months to go?" Dusty flushed hotly when she realized how loud she'd been. "I'm sorry, but I thought you were ready to go at any second. And did you just say babies?"

"Four." Dusty sat down and tried to think what it would be like to have four babies. But Kala laughed. "You should have seen the look on your face. It was both full of panic and terror at the same time. What do you think Riss is going to say when he finds out about them all? I'm taking bets, and most are saying that he already knows. I don't think he does."

"You're going to tell him before you pop them, right?" She was assured that telling him was on her list of things to do. "I can't...four babies. Then four toddlers, and then teenagers? I don't think I'd want to be in your shoes when it...well, hell when it comes to buying shoes. Do you know what they are?"

"All boys. And they'll be like the rest of us. Magical." Dusty nodded and thought of how safe they'd be if some evil prick came gunning for them. When Judith laughed she looked at her.

"I can read your mind, remember?" Dusty had already figured out a couple of days ago that she needed to curb her thoughts when around these women. But she still didn't know how she felt about that. "I won't hurt you when I look, but there are times when I get the real answers instead of the ones you think I want to hear."

"I...." Dusty thought of speaking with her in her mind and was surprised when she felt the connection. *I've been so worried about you guys since I brought this jerk here. The babies will be all right, won't they? I would never forgive myself if anything happened to you guys, and worse if it happened to someone, a lot of someone's, that are so innocent.*

*They will be fine. We all will. The power of working together and knowing our enemy makes things so much better. And you didn't bring him anywhere. He was here before you were a part of this family.* She started to tell her she wasn't a part of anyone's family when Judith cut her off. *You are now. As soon as we took you into our confidence and told you who we were and what we were, you became family.*

As they moved out of her new office she thought of Galin again and wondered if he ever thought of her as his family. Shaking her head at her stupidity, she got into the car and let them take her along. Kip was already at the restaurant when she got there. And she knew immediately something had happened. The look on his face made her want to pull him into her arms and hold him. She knew that keeping him safe was nearly impossible in a situation like this, but she would try.

"Can I tell you later? It's not that bad, but I need to wait until later." She nodded and he hugged her. It was the first one he'd given her without being asked for it since he'd moved in with her. "I want steak for dinner."

And throughout the entire meal she kept a close eye on him and the rest of the group. Dusty was suddenly afraid for all of them. Because no matter what they said, she had brought this on all of them.

# Chapter 7

Markum hurt. Badly. He'd been abused daily for the past several days and he was sure that he looked it. His mirrors, like most of the reflective things he'd had in his room, had been covered by him after the first day. The sex wasn't that bad, but it was painful. And his lordship took great pleasure in giving him as much pain as possible.

Today had been particularly bad. At the first, anyway. He'd been summoned for his punishment and had been held down while two woman had sucked his cock but not let him release. He has hurting so badly with the need to come that he said nothing when his lordship had taken him into his mouth. The heat alone was enough to make him shrivel a little, but the pleasure of being sucked off by one so good at it had Markum coming down his throat in seconds. Then the tables had been turned and he'd had to suck his lordship's cock.

He had a thick, long cock. Everyone who had seen it wondered how a man so well-endowed ever got his cock into anyone. But when he'd flipped him over, after several minutes of Markum sucking him off, and entered him, Markum knew what few others did. His lordship's cock was an illusion and was no bigger than anyone else's dick.

When he slammed into him from behind, Markum had been so disappointed by the feeling that he'd actually turned to see if it was the same cock. He'd been hurt badly for his curiosity.

"You'll keep your mouth shut, or so help me the next time you come into this room, you'll be dead." Markum nodded and said nothing as he was fucked harder for his indiscretion. When he came, his lordship called for a whip and beat him harshly for over an hour before he left him. Five minutes later Markum was being picked up by one of the guards and taken to his room. It was there that he finally got fucked by the cock he wanted. The guard was full of surprising ideas when it came to sex. The man had left him not only satisfied but actually looking forward to more of the same. Markum was nothing if not practical.

Now he lay there alone and his body was slowly healing. He knew that by morning he'd be mostly healed, but it was taking him longer and longer to do so. The more abuse he endured, the harder it was becoming to recover from it. And he was sure that was his lordship's plan.

He looked up when he heard the ding of his monitor. It was the only way he'd been able to keep tabs on the boy and his aunt, as he was no longer able to simply go to the other realm and spy on them himself. By installing a monitor that watched only them he'd been able to keep better track of them, but there were still long periods of time when he would not have a clue where they were.

The boy was with his aunt. Going to the monitors on the wall, Markum pulled up the first view and stared at the people around the table. Most of them he knew and a couple he did not. But he almost didn't recognize either the kid or his aunt. A week had made a great difference in them both.

She looked…well, she looked as if she were glowing. And the boy looked like he'd just been laid. He watched them interact with the others, laughing and smiling. It was enough to make him ill. The longer he watched them the more he wanted to go to their world and murder them both. No one could be that happy all the time without some sort of magic to do it. Humans were generally, in his opinion, a very sad lot. But just as he was going to turn off his monitor, he saw it.

"Mother fucking shit." He paused the view twice to make sure he was seeing it right. "Mother fucking monkey balls. They're dressed."

He'd seen the chain twice, of course, but never put it with a medallion. Now it seemed that someone from higher on the food chain was trying to protect them. Markum started to go and tell his lordship and paused.

"He'll take me again." While the thought of sex normally excited him, he looked down at his body. Markum suspected what he looked like beneath his robe and went into his room to look at his body. Pulling the drape off the mirror, he looked at himself fully for the first time since his punishment had begun. It was much worse than he'd thought, and a good deal more…the scabs on his body would leave large scars that would mar his otherwise perfectly formed body.

In a few words, Markum knew that he looked like raw meat. His chest was so red and wounded he could see his ribs. Several of them were burned as well, leaving his bone showing through the muscle so that he resembled a skeleton. His arms were also burned, and he'd had to tie some of his skin to his arm or have it flap at his chest, hurting him more. His legs looked like he'd been stripped of all his skin except for the parts right over his knees. And even those looked like he'd been dragged behind something moving fast and his flesh peeled away. But it was his face that looked the worst. Oh, his lovely face.

His left cheek was burned and nearly gone. His teeth and gums were visible and his tongue, when he wanted, could poke though the opening and wiggle. It was burned as well and he tried his best not to remember how that had happened. His left eye was there but it was milky and dead for all intents and purposes. He'd wondered lately why he'd been unable to focus on things and thought it was a trick with someone's magic, not his eyes. Markum turned to his right and looked at his face from this angle. It was sickening to see how so much fun could leave one so damaged. His hair was completely gone on this side, as was his ear. In addition to the burns and open wounds, his face leaked pus from his eyes, and he thought that some of that even had worms in it. Markum was a mess. No woman or man would find him attractive. Nor, he feared, would anyone want to have sex with him in the other realms.

Wrapping his robe around him again, he made his way to his bed and lay down. Now that he'd gotten a better view of his body, he was more depressed than ever. As he lay there thinking of his woes and issues, he thought of the woman and his plans for her when he finally got her and the boy. And he would, it was just a matter of time now.

She was going to help him to gain favor with his lordship. A beauty like her would have him salivating for her, and Markum would gladly hand her over. For a price. There was a great deal to be had for a virgin, and more

116

when she was as beautiful, by human standards anyway, as this woman was. Markum thought of her naked and tied to his lordship's bed when he returned with her. His cock, sore and battered, actually stirred. He was frightened that if he had that happen much, it would surely fall off and he'd be in really bad shape.

"She'll be laying there with all her glory spread before him. Her pussy will be wet with her juices and her nipples will be peaked hard and stiff for him. The moment he sees her he'll grow his thick cock from his body and take her hard and fast before spilling his seed into her belly. I shall be there to watch this, too. Helping her to accept him in all his glory."

Markum had come up with his plan when he'd seen her in the shower. She'd been washing her body with a large sponge, and all he'd been able to think about at the time was his hand being the sponge and touching her the way it had. By the time he'd come five times just watching her clean herself for her daily activities, Markum had come up with the idea that she could save him. Then after his lordship was finished with her, Markum would take her to his bed and fuck her until she couldn't stand, much less move. He looked down at his raging cock and wondered if the thing ever hurt enough not to stretch from his body.

Markum closed his eyes and thought about the human's pussy, and felt his cock grow harder. He'd never had a human before and wondered how much better it would be with one. He was thinking of licking her deep with his tongue when he felt someone take him into their mouth. Looking down, he nearly cried out when the pleasure bitch from the throne room moved over his body so that her hot body was over his face.

She wasn't like the human, he was sure of that. Her pussy was that of a woman, of course, but she also had a cock to be a pleasure source for whoever wanted her. Markum played with her until she came, then tossed her off him. She stood staring at his cock like she was starved.

"I'm sore and you wish to make me hurt more." She shook her head and licked her lips. "I want you gone from here. You've gotten your pleasure, now get out."

"I wish to give you some as well." She grabbed his cock and fisted her small hand over him as she moved to her knees. "My body can heal yours if you would let me."

Markum was deep into her throat when she cupped his balls. Even as sore as he was, he could feel his balls tighten to his body, readying for his release. As soon as she rammed her fingers up his ass, she bit down into his dick so hard that he thought she'd bitten his cock off. But he felt the power of her bite, her magic as she began to heal him. His coming this time, hard and quick, nearly made his eyes roll to the back of his head, never to return.

When she let him go, Markum stared at her. She'd healed him. No small feat, either, for as badly as he'd been hurt. When she started to stand, he reached for her and asked her why she'd done it.

"He had no right to harm you." Markum wasn't sure what to say, as no one in all his life had ever thought he was in the right of anything. Ever. "You will heal so much faster. When he comes on you, it will burn slightly but not into your skin. I will come back...if you please, I will come back every night to help you should he be too harsh on you. You have given me pleasure before you took your own. No one, not even another pleasure bitch, has done that for me."

Markum nodded and watched her go. He felt as if he was going to make it now and got up to look into the mirror again. All his wounds were healed, and the best part, he thought his dick looked bigger too. As he started to dress, he thought about going to the other realm and getting the girl and boy now, but decided that he'd wait for a few more days. No sense killing them so quickly now. Markum went to bed with a new sense of worth and slept the sleep of the dead.

~~~

"How much longer do you think to have him suffer?" Boss looked up from his paperwork when Michael spoke. "He is not paying as much attention when they are in the same room as I would like. I fear for her."

"I have others looking in on Kipling when they are together. It is why I have two watching them both, her and Kipling, at the same time. And you worry too much." Michael nodded and sat down. Boss waited, knowing that there was more to this unannounced visit than his concern for Dusty. "She is...I think that the medallion you have given her is going to keep most of the demi-gods away, but I still fear for them. Is there more I should know?"

"There is. You know that I do not tell you everything, Michael. Your mind could not take it all in." Boss waited, trying to think of how to tell him of his plan without upsetting the man. Lately it had been a battle not to share as much as he wanted for fear of making the man upset. And Michael upset was a gloriously wonderful thing, but dangerous for most. "She may be hurt very badly before this is finished if he does not do something soon. I almost hate to do it to her, but she will be stronger for it. They both will. Galin must...he loves her, but knows it not as yet."

119

"She is strong now. I fear for the person who tangles with her. I do believe she is stronger than the other two women. Scary too. Did you know that she can do things that...her mouth is most caustic as well?" She was but Boss said nothing. "I would hope that there is soon to be a reckoning between her and Galin. He is not looking well at all. I see worry lines where there were none before, as well as his rest is not peaceful."

"As I have said, he is in love with the girl but does not know it as yet. I do feel for him. When it hits him he will not take it lightly. His love for her and Kipling will be more than you can imagine." Michael still sat and Boss decided to change the subject. "Did you hear how Riss took the news of his children? It was wonderfully funny. I do not believe I've seen a person, human or otherwise, who turned that particular shade of green. I think I might use that color for something someday."

Boss laughed when he thought of it. They'd been sitting at one of the tables in the great hall on the training yards when Riss put his hand over his wife's belly. He had a look of pure horror on his face when he felt the child move violently beneath his hand. He looked at Him as if to ask Him if it were human or not. Instead of answering him, Boss had looked at Kala.

"It is past time you told your husband of the child you carry. It is going to be enough of a shock to him to find out what it is, much less what it will look like." Riss had stood up so quickly that he nearly had knocked Kala from the chair. "Or I can tell him."

"The baby is...it is not well?" Riss sat down again and pulled Kala into his arms. "It matters not what is wrong with him. I will love him as much as you do and we'll be happy together."

"There is nothing wrong with any of them." Riss had nodded at Kala, then frowned. He asked her what she meant by any of them. "Yeah, you heard me, any of them. All four of them."

"Four? You are having four children?" Kala nodded and Riss stood up and backed from her. "Four is a great many children at one time. How will that be...? What will...? I am not prepared to be the father of four children. Perhaps it would be best if you were to have only one."

"Well, it's a little late for that, dumbass." Kala had stood up then and everyone at the table stood as well. Not to protect her, but to move out of her way. She was on fire with her anger and Boss had enjoyed every second of her wrath. "Just how the hell do you expect me to put three of them back? Up your dick perhaps? Because if you say the word, I'll try my damnedest to put them there. You're not prepared? Let me think on how to prepare you for standing around while I have four of your children. Let me think how my suffering through the labor while you hold my hand can prepare you. You'll be lucky that I even let you touch me again after this. Of all the stupid...put them back? I'd like to put you back where you came from."

Boss had tried his best not to laugh out loud, He truly had, but the expression on Riss's face and him cupping his manhood had Boss laughing so hard that He'd broken the chair from shaking. And when He'd been helped to His feet, He saw Kala going after Riss with a spoon and had visions of her scooping out a child and shoving it inside of him. It had been all He could do not to fall onto His face yet again. He looked at Michael when he laughed as well.

"He is happy now?" Boss nodded, wiping at the tears that streamed down His face. "I should hope so. The poor man would have been hard pressed to placate her after all of that. And you laughing like a loon more than likely did not help. You should have left them to their argument."

"Nay, it did not help, but I would not have missed it for the world. He deserved her wrath for his ill-chosen words. But it made me feel decades younger." When Michael smiled, Boss decided it was time to bring him into the plan. "He will tell her he loves her by the end of the week if everything goes as I have planned. If he only admits it to himself, I will be greatly satisfied. Galin is a good man and will make her happy once he has gotten his head out of the sand and sees what is before him. And she will give him so much more than he can ever give her. The love of a woman, human or otherwise, will make a man richer than any amount of money ever can. And to have one trust you…well, there is nothing greater I believe."

"I hope it works out for them both. He is stubborn, to say the least." Boss nodded his agreement. "I do hope that young Kipling will be happy with Galin as the male in his life. The boy deserves so much. They suit, the two of them. The need to be loved by Kipling will give Galin a warmer heart than one of his own could have, I think."

"He will come to call him Dad before this is finished, and Dusty Mom. He just needed a shove in the right direction, and they have given it to him." Boss leaned back in His chair. "He is to make an announcement tonight. Should you like to see it? You will love it as much as the rest will. Of this I promise you."

"I would very much like to be there. What sort of announcement does he have? He had been…. You are not going to tell me, are You?" Boss shook his head as he brought them both to the kitchen of Dusty's house. "You are not nice at times; I should like to point that out to You."

"I know. But it is so much more fun to watch the expressions on the faces of people when they are not privy to things that only I know. Surprise, as you know, has its rewards as well." Boss took a seat at the table just before a key could be heard in the lock of the door. "Now sit down and be quiet. I do not wish to disturb the telling."

They came into the house and he could see that they were both relaxed as much as they could be under the circumstances. Dusty was a little tense, but he was sure it wasn't from the dinner and company of tonight, but the story that she had been waiting all night to hear of. When she moved to the living room with Kipling, He and Michael did as well. When everyone was seated, Kipling stood to pace.

"I have never been to a school that listens to you before." Before Dusty was able to comment, Kipling raised his hand to stop her. "It's a good thing Aunt Dusty, not bad."

Boss knew the exact moment when Dusty realized that Kipling had called her aunt. He could see the pride on her face and the love that she had for the boy. There was never any doubt about these two making it, but he had his doubts about the protector that stood behind her as she sat there, stunned. Galin was falling hard.

"I have been asked by the principle to participate in the state spelling bee. And she also wants me to ask you if I can take the placement tests to put me into a higher grade." Dusty sat there for several seconds, and Boss saw that her silence was hurting young Kipling. Before he could make his presence known, however, she finally spoke.

"You can spell that good? Well of course you can…your mom could too. I've never seen a woman who could spell anything like she did and not even know the definition of the word. Did you know that when she was in high school, just before she told us about you, that she was supposedly the greatest speller in the world? She told us almost daily how wonderful she was. And she was slated to go to the state spelling bee as well." Kipling's chest puffed out as Dusty continued. "She was so excited to go…to be asked to go…that she walked around with a dictionary for days just spelling words she just put her finger on. I was so sick of hearing her spell everything I'd say to her that I took to sleeping on the couch."

"Did she win?" Instead of answering him, Dusty got up and moved to the tall bookshelf near the television. She walked over to Kipling and handed him a small box. With trembling fingers he opened it and pulled out the beautiful pin with the word CHAMP on it.

"She thought it was lost. I found it when she left home right after we found out about you. I don't know why I even kept it, but it's been up there on that shelf since I moved here. I kept thinking that someday I'd give it to her, but…but I didn't. I'm glad that I didn't now. I can give it to you and that's just as perfect." She helped him turn it over and let him read the back. "She was the champion that day to all of us. Mom was so proud of her that she cried all the way home."

"And my dad? Was he there?" Dusty shook her head at Kipling and Boss waited for her answer, but Kipling was a good deal smarter than he'd thought. "He didn't hang around after she told him about me, did he? I guess she never could pick someone that would stay with her."

"No, she...I'm not sure what happened to him in the years after high school, but right after you came here, I looked for him." Kipling looked panicky and she assured him with a pat to his leg. "Not to get you to go to him—that was never going to happen—but because...I don't know, I thought he should know. But a few years ago he was in a boating accident that took his life and that of his new wife. He'd been happy by all accounts. And if you want to know the truth, I don't think he ever knew about you. Rose was...she left telling us she'd told him, but when I looked for him, by all accounts he was a very nice man."

Kipling tried to give the small medal back to Dusty but she told him it was his. As he fingered the pretty box, Boss knew that he was going to ask about something that had been bothering him for weeks now.

"You had to sell everything, didn't you? I mean, even all the stuff that wasn't worth all that much to anyone but me." She nodded and he nodded as well. "I figured it out when I answered the phone the other day. The guy said that...he said that the auction hadn't brought enough in and that you still owed about four grand of the bills."

"I'm sorry you had to find out that way, Kip. I never wanted you to know how bad things were there. But I did manage to get a few of your things for you. A few framed pictures and some of your books." She went to the closet and pulled out a large but still puny box and handed it to him. "The guy I had at the auction for me said that while nothing was going very high, someone must have trashed some of the things they didn't think would sell. I'm sorry. But he's going to ship the rest, a few things he was able to get, to us soon. I wanted to get all of it back, but there just wasn't any way I could get it and bury your mother too.

You don't know how sorry I am for that. I just didn't have the money." Kipling nodded and Boss felt his love for these two grow more.

"The guy told me that you paid off the hospital bill because they wouldn't let you take her body until you did. He said that Mom had some big bills there." Dusty nodded and moved to take the boy into her arms. "I'm really sorry, Aunt Dusty, about the way I treated you when you tried to help me. I swear to you, some of the things I said to you weren't true. I never hated you. Neither did Mom."

"I know, honey. I know." They sat there for several more minutes before he and Michael left them. He'd seen Galin watch the two of them with love, and wondered how much longer the man would suffer before he admitted to himself what everyone around him could see. He was in love with Dusty McGee.

"I would ask that tomorrow you make sure that there are plenty of people around Strategize and around young Kipling." Michael nodded and looked concerned. "Markum will make a move, and I'd like for Dusty to see how it is when they band together. He will be there sooner than we had hoped, but she will be safe so long as we…I love the woman too, you know."

"You do. I can see that. She will see us at our best." Boss nodded, and when Michael left He looked at His wall of pictures. The one where Markum made his presence known in a very loud way showed a great deal of blood as well as a broken body. It was one of the first images He'd printed when He figured out how. He knew who would be harmed tomorrow and hated it, but it would be just fine in the end. Valyn would recover soon enough and his induction into the Mystic's would be set. Time would tell if his soon to be wife would be a better woman for meeting Valyn or Valyn a better man for meeting her. He thought the man would be lucky if he only knew half of what she'd bring him.

# Chapter 8

Galin watched Kip like he did every other morning, and it took him several minutes of him not getting dressed for school for Galin to realize it was a Saturday and not a school day. When Dusty came into the room with him, getting a cup of hot tea and sitting by Kip, Galin felt his heart take a hard tumble.

"Have you decided if you want to go with me or not?" Kip nodded at Dusty and she smiled. Before Galin could convince Kip to stay home rather than spend the day with his aunt, they were making plans for the day. "I have three projects I have to complete today, then I want to talk to you about a job."

"A job? Doing what?" He frowned. "Are you going to make me sweep the floors or something? I hate using your vacuum. That sucker makes more noise than this guy I knew at my other school did when he snored. Boy, could he snore like the dickens. If you can't afford a new one, I'll go in halves with you for it."

"No. And I'm aware of the noise the thing makes. It's why it's here and not at the office. Denise swore that if I didn't get rid of it, she'd quit. And I need her more than I need less noise when I sweep. No, I want to hire you as a proofer." Dusty got up and missed the look of pure joy on Kip's face. But Galin saw it. Then he looked crushed the next moment.

"You want me to read over your stuff to make sure it's spelled right then?" She nodded and Kip picked up his spoon to play with his cereal. "I guess I can do that."

"I'll pay you." She said this to him with her head in the fridge. Galin could see that Kip didn't really believe her but he wanted to. When Dusty turned to look at Kip, it was as if she knew what he'd been thinking. "I really will pay you. And weekly too. Scale as a matter of fact. Do you know what that is?"

"You pay me what you think its worth for me to find out you've run a spell check on everything. If you want me to go and work for you, I will." She shook her head and sat down across from him. "It's okay, Aunt Dusty. You don't have to—"

"It's ten bucks an hour in cash. You get that every payday so long as you show up to work with me on Saturdays and maybe run for lunch for me when I forget to stop. I'm serious, Kip. It's a real job. I need you to keep me from making a mistake like this one."

The sheet of paper slid across the table and Kip turned it so he could read it. When he looked up from the paper, Galin read it over and over without seeing whatever it was they had seen. It wasn't until Kip spoke that he got it.

"It 'your' not 'you're.'" Dusty nodded. "Did you do this for a customer? Or did you search for it to prove something."

"You're very untrusting today, but no, a customer brought it to me yesterday. He was pleased that I'd caught it as quickly as you did. That's why he hired me. And I'm hiring you. Sometimes, and I mean a lot more than I'd like to admit, things get by us at Strategize that we don't catch until it's almost too late. I think it's a matter of seeing it too much. You'd be fresh eyes for us. I talked to Denise and she's excited too. She said she'd save a fortune in having to redo emails she has to send out for me. I never see them but she said she does." Kip nodded and stared at the paper a little longer. "What else do you see?"

"They spelled their name wrong. Unless they meant to be called Printter's Ink. There is only one 't' in the word." She came around to Kip's shoulder when Galin did and he felt her beside him like she'd touched him. He wanted to pull her into his arms and kiss her, hold her, but knew that it was never going to happen. But her laughter made him pull back until he realized she was laughing at the ad again.

"I never saw that one and I wonder if the client did. I need to look this up when we get to the office. That is simply too funny if that isn't the way they spell it for real." They were both still laughing when they got into the car an hour later. "I can't wait to have you look over some of the things I'm doing for Judith. I hope I spelled my name right, too."

There were so many people in the area around Strategize that Galin felt his wings want to stretch from his body and protect both Kip and Dusty. He moved along with them both, glad now that they were together instead of him at home with Kip. When a little after ten Judith showed up, Galin was glad that she'd brought Agon in as well. He spoke to the protector when he had a chance.

"There are a great many people here today." Agon said he'd noticed that as well, and instead of dropping Judith off today he'd decided to come inside with her. "I think there is something going on. And I can feel something not quite right in the air. Do you think that Boss sent them here because He knows something?"

"He knows everything and you know that. But you are correct, I felt it too. And I've called in Riss and asked him to bring in a couple of trainees from the compound as well." Galin watched as two underlings, subjects of a smaller demi god, moved along the walls of the building. He told Agon about them.

"I didn't know you could see them. That's fantastic. How do you do it?" Galin didn't know and watched as two more moved along the building. "How many do you see?"

"Six. And there are two more stationed right outside the doors. That usually means that someone important from their world is coming here. They usually show up as extra security for some reason." Agon nodded and told Galin to keep him informed. "I will. But you must watch Kip if something happens. I'm going to protect Dusty. I know that Kip is my responsibility but I need to know that she is safe as well."

"I will. But you must know that you will be in trouble should you do this." Galin nodded. "You should think hard, my friend, about why you are willing to do this when you know the trouble it will bring you. I think you will be pleased with the answer as much as she will."

A few minutes later Riss and Valyn showed up as well. With them were two more protectors, and they looked a little nervous. Galin wanted to tell them to bring in someone more experienced, but knew that this would be good training for them. He only hoped that they didn't get in the way when something went down. It was no longer a concern of Galin's that something *might* go wrong, but when. He watched the walls and doors for something to happen.

When the man showed up, it was all Galin could do not to laugh. It wasn't Markum, or at least not him alone. The man who was with him was a demon that he'd dealt with before. Anthony was a horse's butt. When he moved through the portal at the door and was in the building, it was as if every protector within a few dozen yards was put on alert. Galin spread his wings and so did the rest of them. Anthony hissed at him.

"I'm alone, protector, and you are making me nervous. I came to see what the fuss is about. There are a number of your men here and I only came to see what was happening." Galin said nothing as the demon fussed with his long robe of velvet. "As you can see, I'm alone save for this idiot. He told me about this and I came to see what he thinks is something amazing."

"You've said that. Several times now. But you're not alone and you know it. There are as many as a dozen of your minions scrabbling around this room to do your bidding, and we both know that they were here long before you were. Now tell me what you're here for." Anthony grinned and his hot breath fanned over Galin's face. Not only did his hot breath spill from his lips, but the putrid smell of death as well. "Does your boss know that you've come above ground? I'm betting that he has no clue that you have gone against his wishes and did this with that simpleton."

"Markum? Yes, I do agree with you about him being stupid. But my boss…he, unlike your own boss, does not have to know every little detail of our lives. And as for my men being here before me, have you seen the group that stands behind you?" Anthony took a step toward him and

Galin felt his body respond in kind. His wings spread out wide and far and he knew the men and women behind him did the same. "You are going to be hurt, little man, if you do not back down now."

"I'm not afraid of you." To prove his words rang true, Galin pulled his wings into his body just a little closer. He could tell that he'd confused Anthony by his move and smiled at him. "What do you want? And no more of those stupid lies you think will get you out of trouble. Tell me."

Anthony looked at Dusty as she sat at a conference table with Judith and Kala. Dusty didn't know that there were demons in her office, but the other two women knew. And Galin was grateful that they were keeping Dusty out of it. The women were talking about some event to have more people come and see how they could help them get jobs. Kala was talking a mile a minute, something she did when she was excited or afraid about something, he'd noticed. Galin looked at Anthony.

"I come for her. And the boy if I can get him. They would make a nice addition to my harem, don't you think?" Galin said nothing but made sure he was between the demon and Dusty. He could see that Agon protected Kip along with a few other protectors, so he felt a little better.

"You're not getting her. She's not leaving here with anyone but me." Anthony laughed and reached out his hand, and Galin drew his sword from the air when heat started to form at Anthony's fingertips. "You touch her and I'll kill you myself."

"Such brave words for a man who has given her up for no reason. Did she not meet with your expectations, Galin the Brave? Or was she not good enough for one such as you?" Galin said nothing as Anthony continued. "My subject here says that the boy is the one we have been searching for. Is that true?"

"You've been searching for this chosen one for more years than I can remember. What makes this kid have anything at all you want?" He didn't take his eye off Anthony as he watched Kip. Sweat poured down Galin's back as he held his sword in front of him. He would cut the man in half if he moved toward either of them, and he was pretty sure Anthony knew it. The demon made no moves, sudden or otherwise.

"No matter. I will take the child then. You've no use for him either, I understand. I would think that you'd be thanking me for taking him from your care. He is nothing more than a small boy. Unless you want to fuck him."

Galin saw the second that Anthony was going to make his move. When he did, Galin sliced out with his sword twice before he heard the screams around him. Never taking his eyes off the man, he knew that the others were caring for the two people that Galin had only just realized meant the world to him. As he sliced through the air again, he also knew the moment that one of his brothers had fallen.

~~~

"Denise, I swear to you, if you don't stop fussing at me I'm going to murder you." Denise finally sat down but Dusty could tell she was on the verge of standing up again. Before she did, Dusty went into the living room, where the man who had taken a sword for her lay bleeding on her sofa. Valyn winked at her and she felt the tears threaten again.

"It's okay love, really it is. It's the most fun I've ever had." Someone snorted and they both looked at Tholan.

She wasn't sure but she thought the man hated her for some reason.

"You would not have been hurt at all had you simply covered yourself with your wings. It is as simple as cake." Three people said "pie" and Tholan glared harder. "Be that as it may, you have wings for a reason. I would think that a man of your experience would know that and use them. Unless you enjoyed being hurt."

"No one enjoys being hurt. But it was fun. I got to be the hero for this lovely lady." Valyn winked at her again. "And she shed some tears for me. I think that's about the best thing ever."

Dusty handed Valyn a glass of some amber liquid and she watched as he drank it down. Kala had told her the more he drank of this stuff the faster he'd heal. She'd thought of getting a funnel and hose and pouring it down his throat, but wasn't sure how that would work. He'd more than likely find some humor in that too. She looked up when Kip came into the room.

He was cooking. And not just a simple grilled cheese as she'd wanted, but cooking stuff. She wasn't really sure what the things on the tray were called, but they smelled heavenly. Taking one off the pretty plate, she popped it into her mouth and moaned.

"If you keep cooking like this, I'm going to be huge." Kip nodded and moved to three other people who were watching over Valyn. Tholan even took a couple of them and thanked him for thinking of him.

"Dusty?" She turned to look at Michael and followed him into the kitchen. There was no one there and she thought it was more because he'd wanted it that way rather than it just happened to be empty. "I should like for you to speak to Galin. He is...he is most upset by the

136

events of the day, and we are having a hard time calming him."

"Why?" She sat down, wondering why they thought she'd have any control over him either. "He doesn't even like me. What do you suppose I can to do calm him down? And for that matter, what does he have to be upset about? Valyn was hurt and he wasn't even there to see it."

"He was there, love, and he protected you by fighting the demon that was set on taking Kipling to his lair. No, Galin is in love with you." She shook her head and started to stand when Galin was suddenly there. Dusty moved away from the table and toward the door when he stepped in front of her.

"I do love you. And I think my heart stopped beating when I thought you were covered in your blood. I knew that it was Valyn's but it still terrified me." She shook her head again and he nodded. "Are you this stubborn all the time, or just when someone tells you that he's in love with you? Here I've gone out of my way to let you know how I feel and you're being...well, being you."

"You can't love me." He laughed slightly and she crossed her arms over her chest, suddenly pissed off. "Well, you can't. He said you were upset. You look just fine to me. What is really going on that you had to have me calm you?"

"I am calm now that I can talk to you. And you calm me more than you can know by simply being you." She took a step back when he took one toward her. "You don't want me to touch you? I've been thinking of...when he tried to hurt you all I could think of was what I would do without you. I cannot live without you any longer, Dusty. I'm so in love with you...I should like to have an argument with you daily just to see the fire in your eyes when you are upset."

"You said you don't want me. And never wanted to marry me. Well, I've decided that I want a husband. Not you, but I want one." He nodded and backed her up more. "You'll need to go away now. I've told you that you're not to be around me."

"I wish to be more than around you, Dusty. I wish to be buried deep within your body. Giving you so much pleasure that you cry out with it." Her heart rate picked up considerably and her breath caught when he cupped her ass and brought her to his body. She could feel his erection and wanted more than anything to touch him. "Do you know what it was like to know you were so near and I couldn't touch you? Know that you were laying in a bed so close to me and not be able to be with you?"

"You don't want a wife." Even to her ears it sounded lame, stupid really, when she wanted him so much. "Galin, you're going to get into trouble again if you don't stop. And as much as I'd like for you to take me, I don't want anyone to get into any more trouble because of me."

"I no longer care what happens to me when I can have you." He kissed her chin, then made his way down to her throat. Dusty was almost embarrassed because she knew that her heart was pounding. "Let me make love to you, Dusty. I want to take you to your bed and have you cry out my name as you release."

"Please." She wasn't sure if she meant please take her or please let her come, but she was suddenly in her bed and he was moving over her. When he took her mouth again, she knew that this was just for now and right now, that was going to be enough. As soon as the thought formed in her head she knew it for the lie that it was.

Dusty was in love with this man, more than she'd ever thought possible.

Her clothes were suddenly gone. Her body on fire for his touch, she moaned each time he touched her with his fingers or his tongue, yet it was never enough. As his body settled over hers, she felt his cock and wrapped her feet over his thighs, and rode him that way until he took her nipple into his mouth and sucked hard.

"I want to tie you to this bed." She nodded and felt silken ties wrap around her wrists and then tighten to the bed. Her legs were opened, and when he rolled his cock over her pussy, Dusty whimpered. The ties around her ankles had her need spike again. He was not just touching her now, but possessing her. Claiming her.

Dusty watched as he stood up, towering over her while he fisted his now naked cock. He looked at her body as if he were pleased with what he saw, and she wanted to please him very much. Dusty watched him as he knelt at the bottom of the bed.

"I have never done this before but I have seen pictures. The man enjoyed himself greatly by feasting on a woman. Would you like that? For me to feast on you?" Dusty nodded and moaned when he ran his fingers over one hip to the other one. "I don't know if I want to drink from you or bury my cock within you. To do either would bring me so much pleasure. I'm thinking you would like that as well, wouldn't you?"

"Yes. For us both to have pleasure." He grinned at her and she begged him again. "Please, Galin. I need to have some relief or I'm going to explode. I feel like you're touching me already. I can't imagine what it's going to feel like when you actually do."

"Hum, we'll have to do something about that then."
He moved between her outstretched legs and stared down
at her. "You're very lovely here. Your curls are wet with
your dew and your womanhood is open for me to see all
of you. I must have a taste."

As he laid down and spread her nether lips open she
tried to press her legs together. To be exposed to someone
so indecently was something new to her. But when he
flicked his tongue over her clit she cried out and begged
him to take her.

"I should think you'd want me to take my time with
you." He chuckled when she cursed at him. "Temper,
temper, love. We have only just begun. This is much
more...fun than I had thought it would be. To make you
beg me, hearing my name on your lips when you are so
close to completion. Would you like to come, Dusty?"

He licked her clit again, sending waves of pleasure
throughout her entire body before he suckled her into his
mouth and bit down. Dusty cried out her release and he
lifted his head when she started saying his name over and
over.

"Take me. Fuck me please. Galin, I'm dying here. I
need my—" Nothing prepared her for the next climax. It
ripped her apart into tiny pieces only to slam her back
together to have her scream out again. He continued to
fuck her with his tongue and fingers through three more
mind blowing climaxes before he lifted his head again.
Her body was covered in sweat and she felt as tightly
strung as a wire. But even with all her releases, she was
ready for more. Needed more from this man.

"You have given me so much of you." He sat up on
his knees and held his cock. "I'm going to take you now,
love. Fill you with my cock until you release again and

again. Then I will take my own pleasure. I want to feel you tighten around me, feel you when you milk my cock with your release."

"I don't know if I can't take much more." He leaned over her, rubbing his cock head over her clit and just entering her with his crown. "Galin, please. Don't tease me anymore. Take me, I beg of you."

Galin slid into her like he had all the time in the world. Every inch he'd stop and withdraw slightly before moving deeper. By the time he was seated as far as he could go, she was crying again, begging for something and sweat pouring from her body.

"I will never get enough of you." She nodded as he moved in and out of her, his body deep inside of her as he suckled at her breast, not touching her anywhere else but her pussy and breasts. "There is not enough time in the world for me to explore you properly."

"Let me go." The bands were gone almost immediately and she wrapped her arms around his neck. Her legs were slightly sore from trying to wrap around him, and she smiled when she was finally able to lift them to curl around his body. "Fill me, Galin. I want you to come now, come with me please."

His release seemed to be explosive. He cried out twice as he pounded into her deeper than he'd ever been. When he lifted her ass up, his body slamming against her clit, she held onto him as she came again and again. Galin dropped over her even as her body was coming a third time, and Dusty felt her world seem to fade then come back into sharp focus.

She tried to hold onto him, knowing that at any moment someone was going to come and take him from her again. Holding onto him for as long as she could,

Dusty almost cried when she felt sleep taking her. Her heart wasn't going to be able to stand him not being with her after this.

"I have you." She nodded, unable to speak to him over the pain in her heart. "Dusty, I'm not going to ever leave you again. This I swear. And as soon as I can move, I'm going to have Boss marry us. Properly. But I'm not going to leave you again. My heart...my heart can't take that sort of pain again. I love you so very much, my heart overflows with it."

"You don't have to marry me. But please don't leave me." He kissed her cheeks and she looked up at him. "You said you loved me; do you really?"

"I think I have forever." He sat up, resting his head on his hand. "You're very lovely all tousled as you are. I've never noticed the spray of freckles that dances over your cheeks, or the small scar that you have on your nose. I think that you must have been a wonderfully adventurous child when you were little."

"My mother used to tell me that she named me Dusty after the creep she'd had a fling with after Rose's dad died. I think Mom was the reason Rose was like she was. From giving her everything she ever wanted because her father had stayed around for a while. He was...different, from what she used to tell Rose and me. And he loved them like they were the only people in the world, I guess. I sort of got left out in that department. Which I was sort of happy for. It meant that it didn't hurt me so much when she favored her over me."

"She also made you what you are by not giving you things. You are a very strong and independent person because of it, and very successful as well. The fact that you have come through all this without much in the way of

emotional scars is because of what you were growing up."
She nodded and he smiled. "You haven't said how I look
after you have drained me so thoroughly. Do I look as
sated as you are? I feel it even if I do not."

"You're not so bad...." She giggled when he tickled
her. But she knew that there were things they needed to
talk about. Like the people in her house when they'd
disappeared. "Galin, where are the people that were here
when you...when we...?" She flushed hotly when she
thought of what they'd just done. And in the middle of the
day, of all things.

"They have gone home, and it was suggested that Kip
go with Riss and his wife for the night. He is safe with
them. As if he were here with me." She nodded, knowing
that they really loved her nephew and would never allow
anyone to hurt him. "Valyn has also gone to his home. He
will rest there for a few days with someone pampering
him. He will, I believe, milk this for a while longer than
necessary. But I owe him and will let him go for as long as
he wants."

"He stepped in front of me when some kind of
monster tried to take me. I don't know if I will ever be able
to repay him for that. I've never...he could have died."
Galin shook his head and told her he was immortal like
him. Then he held her closer. "What was he, that man who
came for us? And what was he doing here? Surely
everyone knew he was coming. I saw...most of them I
could see, though I don't think I should have. And I was
nervous because of the way Kala was acting. She's very
talkative when she's trying not to be afraid, isn't she?"

"Yes she is. And she babbles as well. But the man,
Markum, came to take you or Kip to give to his master.
His master, Anthony, was...I'm not sure he actually

believed Markum, but he did come to see you. At least that's what he said. And he claimed that Kip was the boy they've been searching for. There is no such boy, but that idiot Markum will try and convince everyone he meets there is one." Dusty looked at Galin to see if he was kidding or at least exaggerating a little. "I would never lie to you even if I could. I will tell you the truth forever now. He came here to take you back with him to gain favor with his master. If not you, then he would have been satisfied with Kip."

She tried to work in her mind what he meant. Dusty understood that it had to do with sex, or whatever they might call it where this person was from. But to be so uncaring about the entire matter made her a little sick to her stomach. Not to mention pissed off. She wanted to find the men and hurt them badly.

"Will he be back? This Anthony person, will he be coming back here soon with Markum? I'd very much like to…I'm not prone to violence, but I would learn to be that way for a chance to show them what happens when you fuck with my family." Galin nodded. "And the next time, will he have more…I guess minions with him? People to do the dirty work?"

"He will have an army." He pulled her close as he continued, and she was suddenly afraid of the truth that he'd tell her. "And Anthony was killed. His death will have repercussions that will be felt for a long time, lifetimes. Markum will pay for his death, and so will many others."

# Chapter 9

Markum barely made it to his room before he dropped to his knees. Anthony was dead. And Markum knew that he was going to have to pay the price for his death. It could not have gone more terribly wrong if he'd planned for it to. Anthony was killed by a protector. And Markum knew that in some way, it was all his fault. He had to work quickly to figure out how to blame someone else for this. Or at the very least, make it go away. He wanted to murder the being all over again, but it was too late for that. Much too late for that now.

"I didn't tell him to come with me. That's what I'll say. I said I'd go and he gave me permission but came as well. He demanded." Not entirely true but he had insisted when Markum told him of the beauty. "And as he ranked higher than me, what could I say to stop him? There was nothing for me to do but to bring him along with me."

Nothing. He could have, he supposed, tried a little harder to keep him from going. And maybe if Markum had not hinted so heavily that he might give him the girl when his master was finished with her too. But that was neither here nor there. The being was dead and someone was bound to find out he had just a little to do with it. Those damned protectors.

"That person had to be more of a protector than I had thought. All of them...how did they know we were coming? Who told them to be prepared?" That was what scared him so much, Markum thought to himself. "The man had such power within him that he even frightened me a little. That's why I begged Anthony to stop this madness. I told him it would not end well. He should have listened to me when I tried to warn him."

Truthfully, Anthony's death and the man who had killed him had terrified Markum to the point where he wanted to simply forget the entire thing and come back here to find the next child. Anthony had been so...greedy. And not like Markum was, but in a killing mood kind of greedy. He'd admired it at first, but then things had gone bad, and now...now he had a dead demon on his hands. Markum told himself that what was done was done. But he was so fucked because of it.

The door behind him seemed to be blasted with a bomb, it opened so hard. When it hit the wall and shattered, wood splintered all over the walls behind him and the floor. He didn't need to turn to find out who it was. It would be all over by now that Anthony had died in the other realm and that he had been with him.

Markum fell to the floor and crawled into a tight ball. He was sure the wrath of someone important had come to take him. And he was nearly to his bed when the man spoke.

"Where is he?" Markum didn't answer the being that had stormed into the room with his sword drawn and his body alight with fire. He might have been impressed with the sight he'd made if not for the fact that he was afraid.

"Where is that imbecile? I will run him through for what he has done."

"Done, my lord?" The being in front of him looked down. Markum felt his bladder loosen and he had to cup himself to keep from pissing himself. If there was something more frightening than this, he never wanted to see it. "Who are you looking for?"

"Anthony. Where is he hiding out? I know that you and he went to the other realm. Just tell me where he is so that I may present him before my lord. He is so pissed...you should see how pissed he is. He wants him now." Markum swallowed twice, telling himself that he did not want to see someone that pissed. The being before him—Oscar the Punisher, he thought his name was—answered to one person, and that man was just under the management of them all, Lord Damon. If he wanted to present someone to his lord it could only mean one thing. That Anthony had—

"He will not be returning." *The lucky bastard*, Markum thought. "He was...his life was cut off when a protector hit him with his sword. You know how they are with those things. It's the only thing that can kill one of us. I know that—" He was cut off.

"A mere protector cannot kill a demon. It matters little what the sword is." Markum wanted to point out that he'd thought the same thing but said nothing. "Where is the paragon of strength? I should like to meet a lowly protector who would dare raise a sword to one of my men."

"Lord Anthony did raise his sword first, my lord. In fact, Anthony went there with a small army. His intent was to take a human as his own." The more Markum thought about this, the better he liked it. What was

Anthony going to say about his lies? Nothing. He was dead. And now it was time for Markum to look out for himself. Not that this time was any different, but he was here and Anthony was not. "Not that I condone what he has done, but I do believe that Anthony brought his death to himself. He was most insistent that the human would be his."

The growl made him whimper and Markum curled back into his ball. Before he could think about leaving the room, he was picked up and tossed across the room so hard that he stuck in the hard stone. Markum nearly tried to free himself but decided that he'd be safer, for now at least, hanging where he was. He could not be thrown about if he was already plastered against something.

"You dare judge my men? You would say something about a man who is no longer here to defend himself?" Markum cringed when his lordship came at him again. He knew then that he'd been very wrong in what could happen to him, as he was peeled from the stone and thrown harder against the opposite one. "I will have you boiled with your own guts for that."

"Technically, if you boil me, sire, I will have my own guts already." The blast of heat hit him in the belly. Markum had never learned not to correct his betters, and it was forever getting him into trouble. But was it necessary for them to be so incredibly stupid all the time? Where was he supposed to store his guts while the man put him in a pot? Markum decided that at the next meeting he was going to see if he could have a class set up. Ways Not To Sound Stupid. Markum was thinking of subtopics when pain tore at his body. He screamed again when his cock was pulled hard, and when he reached to cover himself for some protection, he was hit again, this time in the face with heat. He didn't dare look down, sure that the man had torn his cock from his body and would have it for his supper later.

"You are going to force me to kill you if you do not shut your mouth." Markum nodded, not even sure he could speak again with the pain in his face. The being started to pace the room and Markum tried to think how to get out of this. He was just a simple demi-god and he knew that while he was a great deal smarter than the man in front of him, the man did out rank him. But before he could think of the no doubt wonderful plan, the being started talking.

"He will want restitution for this. One of his own was injured. I do not have the men to let go to take his place. Not that any would." Markum started to volunteer himself to whatever the duty was when the being continued. "Death would be preferable to whatever he wants of him. My death too if he has his way. To have had one of my own go and do something so...are there not rules in place for us to keep to? Do we not learn these from the start? We do not take what is not given to us freely."

He moved out of the room and the door hung a little more crookedly on the hinges when he left. Markum waited a full five minutes before he freed himself from the wall. When he was surveying the damage, he heard someone come into the room. He was surprised to see the pleasure bitch. His cock started to harden at the thought of her healing him, but it had nearly been ripped from his body, and he feared it would never harden again, much less still be a part of his pain filled body.

"I cannot." He started to ask her why when she dropped to her knees and bowed her head. "It has been found out that I have helped you before. My master is very angry with me that I would dare heal the likes of you and not him. He said that if I were to come to you again and take so much pleasure from you that he would punish me for the end of my days. You will...I came only to tell you what has happened."

"He's hurt?" She shook her head. "Then I don't see what the problem is. If he's not hurt now, then you can heal me. It's only fair, I think, since you said you'd do it if I needed it. And I won't mind if you don't have any pleasure. In fact, it's okay if you only give me some. I mean, it's the only way you can heal me, right? If you bite me and I come?"

"But he has forbidden it. To give you pleasure would be most...I cannot." Markum shook his head and she looked at him, frowning. "You think that I should defy him?"

"No. I think you should go to him when he's hurt, just like he said, but he only said you should heal him. He's not hurt and I am. It's the way he'd want it if you asked him." Probably not, but he was hurting and would do most anything to be whole again. And to have her suck him off, to have her take him into her mouth, was nearly as good as being fucked by three of the pleasure bitches at once. "If he asks you why you healed me then tell him to speak to me. I'll explain to him that you were doing as I told you. I have a great deal of respect around here, and he'll only beat you because you made me wait. You know that's what he'd want."

She sat on her knees for several more seconds and Markum was afraid. If she didn't heal him, and since it was a being that strong who had hurt him, then he'd never heal this time. He might as well go to the other realm again and pick a fight with the protector that had killed Anthony and let him end his painful life. And if she did heal him, he could have his cock spray down her throat and he'd think of the human again. Smiling, he watched the pleasure bitch as she thought over what he had said.

"I will heal you, but you will tell my master that I have only done this as you have asked? He will not be upset because I have done this if you were to tell him what you've said to me. This is what you are telling me?" Markum nodded and moved toward her. She put her fingers on his cock and he felt the pain lessen. She seemed to be examining him very thoroughly and he was ready to ask her why when she looked up at him. "You will take more than one bite to heal, I think. I will need to do it several times."

"Whatever you need to do. Just heal me, please." He felt her tongue touch his cock and knew real pain. Before he could tell her to leave him alone in that area, she took him into her mouth and bit him hard. Markum was sure that the entire realm could have heard him scream.

~~~

Galin wanted to help her, but she'd told him in no uncertain terms that if he touched her again, she was going to murder him. The fact that he had laughed more than likely didn't help either. But she was so adorable trying to lift the sword and use it like he had.

"You would be better off with a smaller sword." Dusty glared at Michael at his suggestion. "I can fabricate you one if you wish."

"If I have a smaller sword, then I have to be closer to them in order to slice and dice." Michael looked at him as if he didn't understand. Galin tried very hard to simply tell Michael what she meant, but he was afraid of laughing again. This was more fun than he'd thought it would be.

"She means to do this and we shall let her. I think her plan is a good one. The further away she is the better for her." Boss appeared behind her. "And a lighter sword does not mean shorter. Here. Try this one and see how it works for you."

In seconds, less really, Dusty was holding a thinner, lighter sword that seemed to fit her hand better as well. His pommel had been too thick for her and he'd tried to tell her that. But like all things he'd noticed, she was determined to be proficient in this. As her new sword started swinging through the air with a great deal more grace, Boss walked to him. He looked to be finding this whole thing as funny as he. But neither man, he noticed, laughed at her now. The sword would cut them deeply.

"She is very strong willed, is she not?" Galin nodded. "I've never seen anyone have such a desire to win before. Dusty is nothing like the other women that are protectors. I think she will do well with you, and the others will learn from her as much as she will from them. I am glad that you have decided to wed her."

"I'm not sure that it's winning so much as keeping Kip safe. She's has it in her head that she's the only one that can keep him from being taken by Markum." Boss looked at him when he cleared his throat. "I told her that she was immortal now, and she asked me about Kip."

She'd been upset at first, but he explained to her that someday they'd be able to keep him with them forever as well. But he was much too young now and would stay that way if he were to be converted now. While she was still upset, she understood better.

"You will bring her to me for the ceremony soon? I have a wish for you to be wed before the day is out." Galin started to tell Him that Dusty had no plans of marrying him, but wasn't sure how He'd take it. He was still trying to figure out how to get her to say yes.

"I've got it." They both turned back to Dusty when she spoke. She was working with Arryn now and seemed to be holding her own. He was shouting moves to her each time he was able to nick her blade and she was picking up on them very nicely. And Galin thought her the most lovely creature he'd ever seen.

"You need to keep your arm up. That's it, but don't let me see your heart." She moved with him, and each step she took seemed to be planned and precise. "Now, when I attack you, I want you to think of protecting yourself."

"I thought that was what I was doing." Arryn shook his head and looked at Galin. When Dusty turned to look at him, he knew that she wasn't going to be happy about this either. There were times, like this one, that he wished she wasn't so independent.

"He means your wings." She stared at Galin for several seconds before she looked back at Arryn. He nodded once at her before she dropped her sword. As she walked away, he moved to follow her and she stopped and turned on him.

"Don't. Not...I don't want you to touch me." She turned back and moved away from him. "I have wings? And no one bothered to tell me. What if I had sprouted them with a bunch of clients around?"

"You can't." She turned and glared at him and he took a step back. "You can only use them if you think of them or are afraid. You can also use them to protect others, as I have done for you. And as of the night I claimed you, you have all the powers I have."

Dusty didn't look all that thrilled and Galin found he wanted to take yet another step back from her. She started walking away again and he followed, but at a greater distance this time. She didn't have the sword but she could still hurt him. And he was pretty sure there would be no help for him from his friends.

"When were you going to tell me this?" He didn't get a chance to answer her when she continued. "I suppose you were waiting until I was in the middle of a battle or something and you'd go, 'oh, by the way, you can fly around the room like a bird and land on high buildings. And those suckers can wrap around you and save you from being killed.'"

He didn't say anything, not even to point out again that she was immortal. She could do all that, but he didn't think this was the time to point it out. When she got to the end of her property she leaned against the fence post and looked beyond. He could tell she was crying, and he wasn't sure how to comfort her and keep her from hurting him. Galin decided that he'd give her a few more minutes, then he would try to hold her.

"He's going to...this Markum person, he's not going to stop, is he? I know you said there is no chosen one, but he won't stop until he's got some kid, even if it's not Kip. Someone is going to have to kill him, aren't they?" Galin moved up behind her now and wrapped his arms around her waist. "I don't want anything to happen to you guys. It nearly broke my heart when Valyn was hurt, and it was hardly a flesh wound. And I know that he's up and around today, but it's still painful to know that it happened because of me."

"I think he enjoyed it." She snorted at him and he laughed. "Believe me when I tell you, he enjoyed himself. He is still talking about how he took one for the team. I think that most of us, me included, would jump at the chance to do what he did yesterday. Not every day, mind you, but it was a nice feeling to defeat the bad guys for once. And to protect a lovely damsel while doing it."

As they stood there a family of deer walked into the open field. There were other animals as well. Galin could see their watchers as they moved along with them. Each animal, both above the ground and below, would have someone to watch over them. As two of the protectors waved at him, he noticed that Dusty waved back. It was something he'd forgotten she could do. See the others.

"I have this mark on my arm. In the same place you do." He nodded but said nothing. "At first I was a little freaked out...here I have this thing on me that I didn't okay or even know about. But then I touched it."

"I felt it." She turned in his arms and looked up at him. "We are as one, literally. When you are touched, I feel it too. Hurt or in pain, those emotions and feelings are as much a part of me as anything on my body. Your wings, when you see them, will be snowy white and just as full as mine. But now...well, when we are wed, we will each have a part of the other, and one feather from each of us will go to the other. It will keep us safe."

"I don't know if I want to have wings." Galin looked into her eyes as he pulled his free from his body and wrapped them around them both. She looked around them and then back at him. "Is this what he meant by keeping me safe?"

"It is. And no other being, none, will be able to see you when you are thusly wrapped. Boss can, I believe; I've never asked, but no demon can, nor can any other protector. If you are hurt, your wings will hold you safely until you can heal. And because of the magic in them, you will heal much faster anyway. They are to keep you warm when you need it, and if you are protecting someone, they will shield you both from any harm. They are there for you to use, and you should get used to them." He opened his wings and pulled them to his body. "Do it, Dusty. Pull them free and feel them."

He could see that she was afraid. He wasn't sure he'd seen that emotion on her before and was surprised by it. When she closed her eyes, he could feel her wings beneath his hands and moved down to her waist. When they fluttered open, he ran his fingers over the tips of a few of them. The expression on her face had him doing it again. He would never be able to describe the look of pure bliss on her face.

"I can feel that. I mean really feel it. All over my entire body. It's erotic." He opened his wings again when she asked him to and nearly fell over when her fingers slid over him in the same way. "I can feel it. It's like...it's like you're touching me with your tongue. And my body is on fire to have you touch them over and over until I can come."

Pulling her body to his, Galin moved them to their room. This was going to require some exploring and he didn't want anyone to see them. Once they were in the bedroom, he told her to turn around and he moved up behind her. He ran his hands over her entire wing span and then back again. She was panting by the time he finished. And so was he. He'd never felt anything like this before, and wanted to enjoy it a great deal more.

"I want to see what it's like to touch you with one." She turned and he pulled one of his feathers from his wings. "Will your clothing away. I want to explore you with nothing to keep us apart."

Her clothing was gone before he could drop to his knees. Galin was also naked now and his cock was thick with need. But there was time enough for that. He ran the feather over her hips and watched her face. Her entire body reacted to his touch. His own had his cock leaking from the tip, and he watched as she licked her lips.

Galin ran the feather over her entire body, stopping only once to drink from her when her juices slipped down her thigh. She screamed out her release, and all he could think about was having her do it again and again. By the time he was ready to release, she had climaxed thrice. She was also begging him to take her. He wanted her so badly that he had to sit and take several deep breaths before he thought he could move without releasing before they began.

"I should like for you to return the favor." She nodded and he stood up. Before he could hand her his feather, she pulled one from herself and slid it along his cock. He wasn't prepared for the pleasure of it and cried out when she ran it over his tip. Galin had to reach for the bed posts to hold on or he surely would have fallen. He knew that if she did it again, he was not going to be able to hold back.

"Again. Please again." Over and over she teased him, bringing his release just to the edge and pulling back. He might have begged her to finish him, but he was enjoying the pain of this too much for her to do that. When she took him into her mouth, Galin nearly fell back. Nothing had ever felt this good before. And when she cupped his balls and gave them a slight twist, Galin filled her with his seed over and over as he ejaculated down her throat. It wasn't enough. He needed more. He needed her.

He stood holding onto her head for several minutes as she continued to lick him. He was nearly in too much pain to enjoy what she was doing, but didn't want her to stop. When his cock seemed to fill again he told her to move to the bed. But instead of lying on it as he had expected, she leaned over and spread her legs wide for him. Going up behind her, he slid his cock into her sheath and moaned at how deeply he could take her. Holding onto her hips as tightly as he dared, he rolled his hips back and forth until he was so close to releasing again that he almost didn't hear her speak.

"Spank me, Galin." He ran his hand over her lovely bottom and thought about doing just what she said. When she told him again, commanded really, he brought his hand down hard and nearly released when she cried out. He spanked her three more times before she screamed out that she was coming and Galin followed close behind.

Leaning forward, he took them both to the bed. He'd always enjoyed sex with her, but when he'd spanked her and released, he felt as if his body had been taken apart one molecule at a time to be put back together with so much force that he felt...he felt as if he'd been made a new person. He held her to him as he thought about his life with her. Just being with her was more than he'd ever hoped for, but to have her as his wife was something that he felt he needed more than his next breath.

"Will you marry me, Dusty? I should very much like for you to be my wife. Forever. And I will...I know that Kip is a concern for you, but I would enjoy helping you raise him up into a good man. Marry me?"

She yawned and he thought she was too tired to answer him. "If we do this, and I'm not saying yes, but if we do, then I have one thing that I'd ask you." He told her anything. "Don't ever lie to me or keep things from me because you think I won't be able to handle it. I might not, but at least I don't have to worry about whether or not you're keeping something from me. I don't want to have to worry that something will be going on and you've not told me."

"I cannot lie to you or anyone. But I promise you, from this day forward I will keep you informed about everything I know. And if you would like, I'll have the others do so as well. I don't think you'll have a problem with Kala or Judith telling you what is what, but the rest of us will do the same." She nodded and closed her eyes. "Dusty, is that a yes?"

"Yes. I'll marry you. But I'm tired right now and—" He pulled her into his arms and kissed her. She was going to be his wife. Before she could change her mind he contacted Boss and let him know.

*Perhaps you should wait until later before you come to me.*

Galin told him no. *I want her now. It's to be now. Please. She said yes, and if we wait she will think of a hundred reasons why we can't do it. I need her to be in my life.* He thought of the man he was talking to. *If you have time, that is. I do fear, however, that later she might have excuses not only lined up on paper, but in an order of importance as to why we aren't suited. Please don't let her make a list. I don't...could you please see us now?*

In seconds they were both dressed and standing in Boss's office. Galin could see He was having a hard time not laughing at him, and Dusty looked ready to murder him, but he didn't care. She'd said yes and he wasn't going to give her any wiggling room to say no. As soon as Michael entered the room, Boss stood up. It was time…past time, he realized. Suddenly Kip was there and Galin was glad that he'd been brought in for the wedding. He'd have to remember to thank Boss later.

"I have great plans for the men I have chosen. Picking a wife for you, Galin, was a challenge. She needed to be soft and strong, confident as well as a little unsure. A woman that would keep you on your toes." He took both their hands and winked at Kip. "In this, I believe I have not just chosen well, but I have made a perfect match with the three of you. I can only hope that the others will be just as easy."

"Easy?" Michael flushed when they all looked at him when he shouted. "This was not easy. She gave us all a run for our change. I've never seen two people more ill…you two have given me my first headache. Ever. And now you say this was easy? I do not think I can handle much more of this. You might need to give me a vacation when this is finished. Easy is not what I would call this union."

"You'll hold your tongue, my good friend, or I will find you a wife that is more like this one than you can imagine." Michael's mouth closed with an audible snap. "Very good. I knew that you'd see it my way."

Galin had a moment to wonder who else Boss had plans of marrying, and smiled. Whoever they were, he wished them the best of luck and was glad he was going to get to see it happen. And he'd laugh every time one of them balked at the idea of finding a wife. Then Boss spoke again.

"I bring you together not just as man and wife but as a family. My first in the Mystic's. Kipling will grow to love you both as his parents, as I have as my children. I bless you with all that I can and will. You are now man and wife, father and mother, a strong family." Galin kissed Dusty when the rings were slipped on their fingers. He felt a wave of...of power pour over him, and he reached for something to hold onto. It just happened to be Boss.

"Steady now. You'll have your feet under you soon and you'll be fine." Galin nodded and looked for Dusty. "She is fine. Took it harder than you, but she will be fine. Michael is fussing over her now. Kip is helping. Are you able to stand on your own, my son? You still look a little pale."

"I'm fine. I think. What was that? What happened?" Boss winked and Galin was almost afraid to ask again. "You've changed us somehow, haven't you? You've...what have you done and not told us?"

"I have. You are now a part of my Mystic's. You and Riss, with the others, will be training my men from now on. Dusty and the female Mystic's will be hard at work making sure they are taken care of as well." He smiled again. "You were thinking I'd done something else? I assure you that as much as I want to, you are just what you are. Both of you. My pride and joy."

That was somewhat confusing, but Galin didn't want to think about it now. He looked over at Dusty, who was trying to stand, but Michael kept pushing her back down. The man could fuss like an old woman could. More than likely better.

"She's not going to be happy about this. I'm supposed to tell her when something like this is going to happen." As if on cue, she started yelling at Michael. The poor man looked so terrified of her that both he and Boss laughed. "I think she'll be a great trainer. But she's going to have your head for this, and I might just laugh at it. She's a little on the rough side when she feels like this."

"As do I, Galin the Brave, as do I. But I don't fear her. She is going to be just fine. Just fine indeed." They both looked at Kip, who was laughing at his aunt. "As will he. All of you will be just fine."

# Chapter 8

"You dare to tell me what I am to do?" Markum was feeling pretty good except for this fool in front of him. In fact, he felt pretty fucking fantastic. He'd been healed by the time he woke up, and the pleasure bitch had given him the best climax of his life. After she'd gone to rest, he'd cleaned up and decided to go and see his lordship again. But the man could not see what he had.

"You are not seeing the big picture." Markum nearly stood up but stayed where he was. He might be feeling good but he wasn't stupid. "The woman would bring us so much. Not just in fucking her, but can you imagine how many she can bring to us? It boggles the mind."

Damon, his lordship, only stared at him this time. It was on the tip of Markum's tongue to tell him to get his head out of his ass. These beings…they got a little power, and then all they wanted to do was sit back and bask in it. Did no one but him see that if you worked hard at being different than the others, you could have so much more? Apparently not. Markum was beginning to think that he was the only one in this entire realm who had vision; that and any sort of intelligence.

Damon spoke again. "You will stay away from this girl. You will keep to your job and not raise your head or yourself above your position, or I shall make you hurt in ways that the other master did not." Markum started to speak but was cut off. "How you talked Anthony into going with you on this folly I will never know. But I am not like him, and I will take you down if I need to. And don't even try to tell me that—"

"He talked me into going there. I swear to you, it was him, not me." The man glared at him and Markum nodded. "It's true. I only told him what a beauty she was and he decided, all on his own, that he was going to bring her to his bed. How was I to know he was going to be killed by a protector?"

"Because she is married to one, you fool." Damon's voice thundered through the room, echoing back to Markum several times as he stood over him. This being was not as easily duped as Anthony had been. He didn't use sex as a punishment either, but hurt a person with his knives and his blades, more's the pity. Markum watched as he strode back and forth mumbling about rules and pact laws. Markum had heard them all before; in fact, he'd had to take a class about them before he could be promoted to minion.

"You will listen to me, Markum. If you do not, then I will have no choice but to let the other realm have you, and you do not want to know what they do to our kind." He'd seen it first hand and wasn't really all that impressed. Sure they'd killed Anthony, but they cried like little babies when one of them was hurt. He didn't think they could take on someone like him, and he was only a demi-god...powerful and smart, things the protectors were not very strong in. But for now, anyway, he would bide his time.

"Anthony went there without a single blade to protect him. He didn't even take but a few minions there to make sure that we got out safely." Markum nodded, liking this version of the way things went much better than the truth. "I tried to talk him into taking at least a few people, but oh no, he had it in his head he was all powerful. He even told me that he was stronger than you."

"Did he now?" Markum was on a roll and decided that he'd cover his bases all the way around. As he'd realized before, there was no one to dispute his claim. This was way too easy for him, and Markum had always prided himself on finding what was easy.

"Yeah, he did. Even told me that he was going to take the girl to his own bed without telling you that he had her. She is a fine piece of ass. And that boy...you should see him. Prime he is. I think...I could feast on him for days and days just looking at him." Markum thought about telling him what he thought the boy was, but decided that would be for later. No one ever believed him about the boys he'd found, and he was frankly sick of that as well.

"You have an image of this paragon of beauty?" Markum had to hide his smile. Hook, line, and sinker, as his master used to say. "I could care less of the boy, but this woman, she is that beautiful that Anthony would go against me?"

"She is." He closed his eyes and thought of the woman naked in the shower. As soon as he had the image, he projected her onto the wall across from them. "As you can see, she is healthy and would be able to take a good fucking like no other. And her breasts. Don't they look like they're begging you to bite them? And a fine ass she has.

I'm betting you could fuck that pretty pussy of hers while another took her ass hard. This woman is made for fucking...can't you see it?"

Markum noticed that the man cupped his cock. When he started stroking it, Markum showed him the image of her while she washed. She was leaning over in the shower and running a razor over her long legs. She did this over and over as if she knew that someone was watching her and wanted to show them what they couldn't have. Not yet at any rate. He'd have her, and soon too. Even his own cock stirred when she bent again and washed her feet. Her ass was tight and Markum wanted to sink into her so badly he rubbed his own cock while he thought of doing it.

"She is lovely. And you're right about that ass. I could see me coming into her tight hole as soon as I entered her." Markum looked at his lordship and saw that he'd freed his cock. When he started to fist himself, Markum freed his own and watched him while the image of the woman moved back and forth between her nice ass to her hard nipples. A noise from his lordship had him looking at him again. Markum pulled harder on his cock when he saw what was going on not two feet from him.

Two pleasure bitches were sucking him off, and each other too. As one would suck on his thick cock, the other would eat the other's pussy. It was enough to make a grown man cry, there was such beauty in this. The entire time, his lordship watched the woman that Markum wanted in the worst kind of way. Slowly moving up behind one of the bitches that was leaning over her master, Markum slid his cock into her heat as he reached for her cock and jerked hard on the extra appendage until he felt her leaking on his hand. He had his balls fondled tightly when the second bitch grabbed him as she sucked cock. He was pounding into her hard when his lordship roared out his release. Markum came as well but moved quickly back to the floor, hopefully before he noticed him. He was nearly dizzy with his release. It had been quick and hard, but so satisfying as well.

His lordship sat there with his flaccid cock laying on his thigh. Markum wanted to go to him and taste his cum, but was afraid he'd be pushing his luck. The bitches left them, but he could see them just around the throne as they started fucking each other. Markum was hard and hard pressed not to join them as they cried out their own pleasure over and over. Just to watch them eating each other's pussy was enough to have his cock ache again. He wanted to join them in the worst kind of way.

"You'll bring her to me." Markum started to rise to get one of the bitches when his lordship continued. "I will have her in my bed and ready by tomorrow. If you should happen to get the boy too, you may have him. I've no use for a child. And you are to be careful of the protector. As he has taken her to his heart, he will be stronger for his folly."

"And her husband? Do you wish me to kill him? And how much stronger will he be? Like the one who killed Anthony? How will I get her from him if he is, as you say, stronger for it? I've only...I am only a demi-god, sire." Markum tried to look humbled and was sure he wasn't pulling it off. It had been his plan when he'd woke that morning to be given extra powers so he could go and get the woman. And now not only might he get them, but he'd fucked a demons pleasure bitch while he got his rocks off too. It was turning out to be a much better day than he'd hoped for.

"I'll give you what you need when you are in that realm. But it is only temporary. Once you are back in this realm, you will be as you are now." With a flick of his wrist, Markum felt the power surge over him. "You abuse this power or do not get me what I want, then there will be no hole deep enough for you to hide in, Markum. I will make you pay in ways that you'll think that Anthony coming on you would be a good thing."

Markum nodded. He didn't tell the man that he'd found it pleasurable anyway and had been disappointed when he'd not done the same, but he moved out of the room and to his own. It was time to make plans. And if he had to bring the woman to his lordship by tomorrow night, he had to work fast if he wanted to fuck her too. He was not taking sloppy seconds. Moving through the portal that would take him to the other realm, Markum nearly fell over when his new powers took his breath away.

"Now this is more like it." He spread his fingers out and grinned at the power there. He aimed his fingers at a woman standing at the corner of the street he'd come to and watched in glee as she simply disappeared in a puff of smoke. Laughing, Markum made his way to the house where his woman lived and tried to think what to do to her first. He was going to have to fuck her first and foremost. His dick was hurting and he needed relief.

"Just fucking her seems so…well boring. I'm going to…yes, I'm going to tie her to a post and burn her flesh until she begs me to fuck her." Happy now that he had a plan, Markum was nearly to the house when he remembered the protectors. "Damn it. I'll have to deal with them first."

He found the first one standing in front of a building. The woman he was watching was not his woman, but he found her to be pleasing to the eye. Slicing heat into the protector, he reached for the human at the same time. By the time the protector was standing again, Markum was taking her back to his lair and chaining her up with the others he had there. He noticed that one of them was finally awake.

"Hello Jacob. Are you ready to help me now?"

~~~

Dusty was working on her next project when she looked up and saw someone standing near her window. He didn't move when she noticed him, and she was ready to call for Denise when he finally turned to her. She stared at him for several seconds before who he was occurred to her.

"Jacob?" He nodded and held up his hand when she started for him. "I need to call someone to help you. Just...I'm going to call Galin and the others."

"They cannot help me because I am not here." He moved then and she could see that he was sort of transparent. "I am kept in the dungeons of the other realm and have been...there are others here that will need you to come for them. But do not be fooled by the ease with which you get in. He will try most anything to get you into his bed. You will be very safe when you come here. I do not wish for harm to come to you, my lady."

"I will, but I don't understand." He nodded and moved again, and this time she could see he'd been hurt badly and stood up. "I need to get to you. Tell me where you are. I can't stand the thought of you being hurt so badly and not where I can help you. Please, Jacob, tell me."

"You will do so much for us, I think. But now is not the time for you to be heedless of what is happening, but

169

for you to stay focused on the issue at hand, all right? Tell Boss something for me. Tell him that I need him but you must come as well. It will be the only way for all of us to be safe. You will need to think like you always do. Think of what he is saying and who is saying it. Will you?" She nodded and reached for her pen and paper to write down the message to give to Boss. "You will not need that, my love. But I will give it to you."

He moved then. Jacob didn't walk like she thought he would, but seemed to teleport to her. He was suddenly standing in front of her and she wanted to touch him. When he put out his hand she reached for him, and as soon as she touched him, he became solid. Then something powerful surged through her as he told her again to be careful. As she staggered back from it and Jacob, he smiled at her and faded out. She called for Denise just as she hit the floor.

"...stupidest job I've ever had. People coming in here in the oddest ways and making demands on me like I'm working for them and not her." Dusty opened her eyes and looked at Denise as she held her. She didn't know who she was talking about and nearly asked when she snapped at someone just behind her. "You make me come over there and show you how to make a cup of tea again, I'm going to snap your neck."

"Denise, when did you become so violent?" Sobbing, Denise pulled her tightly to her. Dusty wasn't really sure what had happened but let her hold her. She'd been terrified and that was enough. And it felt really good to be held like this, like the woman really loved her. Dusty hugged her back.

"You scared the crap out of me." Another hug before Denise let her go. "You ever do that to me again and I will hurt you. Scared nearly fifty years off my life when I heard you screaming. Then to have you faint dead away like you did. I never seen a body faint before and I hope to never again. I swear to you...and who is the Jacob person?"

"Jacob." Dusty sat up and reached for Boss. *You need to come here right now. Something has happened to my protector.*

Almost as soon as she finished the command, Boss was standing in front of her. Denise screamed again but only stood back. She was either going to have to give her a raise or buy her something really great when this was done. Dusty knew that for so long as she lived, she'd never find someone like her ever again, and knew that she didn't ever want to.

"Jacob was here. He said I was to give you something." But for the life of her she had no idea what it was. "He handed me something. But now that I think about it, I don't know what it was. He just touched me and I fell over. You don't think I lost it when I fell over, do you? Please tell me that I didn't. I don't know what I'd do if we couldn't get to him in time."

"Touch me."

Dusty wasn't sure that was a good idea and put her hands behind her back. There was something so...off about him that made her think he was not well. Or something.

"It is a message that only I can understand. He must have been...I'm not trying to insult you, but he must have been very desperate to have given it to you. I would have thought he'd give it to someone with more...well, just more of everything."

Then Boss did something he'd never been seen doing before; he rolled his eyes at her. "Give it to me, woman."

"He was hurt." Boss nodded and moved toward her. "Will you be hurt by this like I was? If so, then I'd rather you just let me figure it out. There is no reason why everyone should be injured over this."

"That's really nice of you, my child, but impossible. The fact that he gave it to you tells me that you're very powerful; for him to be able to contact you is something else altogether. I didn't plan on that. And that you did not fail to receive it says a great deal for your strength. But the message is for me. I should take it so that I can help him." She started forward when she remembered something else.

"He said that I had to come to the other realm as well. That it was the only way." Boss put his hand down and watched her. She could see the disbelief on his face. Hell, she didn't know what the hell was going on, and she had been there when Jacob had come to her. "You have to let me help you. Jacob needs me."

"Very well." She moved forward and before she put out her hand, Boss pulled her to his body. The surge of heat nearly had her begging him to let her go, but as soon as he did it, she realized they were no longer in her office. "Do not ask me where we are."

Dusty nodded. "I'm to assume we're not in Kansas anymore then?" Boss nodded and she did as well. When he turned to look around, she told him what else Jacob had told her.

"He is a very brave man for what he's done. I cannot…it's not possible for me to see the goings on in all the other realms. When it's not the one I live in then it's like a door is there." Dusty nodded after Boss spoke, already having figured that part out. "When we find them we will—"

"Them?" Boss looked at her questioningly. "Them? You said them as if you already know there are more than just Jacob. How would you know that when I didn't tell you? Do you…are you really Boss?"

"Of course I am. Who would I be if not him? What a stupid question. Of course I'm him. I don't know why…why would you even ask me that?" Before she could tell him she simply didn't trust him, that was why, he shoved her against the wall and put his hand over her mouth. In seconds she could hear someone speaking as they came toward them. Her wings…she wanted to free them to protect herself, but he leaned into her ear.

"You will give us away if you do that. The magic that comes with opening them will have them finding us sooner. And I'm just not ready for anyone to find us. And Jacob did warn you that the trip in wouldn't be as easy as it seemed." Dusty nodded as he continued. "I am going to let you go for now and then leave. But only for a second. Stand here and do not move. I shall come back as soon as I find them."

She wanted to leave herself. Something was going on here that she didn't understand or trust. She would have argued the stupidity of him leaving her alone if he hadn't left her almost as soon as he finished speaking. Dusty leaned back against the hot wall she was standing next to and thought of how dumb this was. Before she started to panic and berate herself on how next time a big boss told her he'd handle it, she'd fucking let him, Boss appeared.

"He is here as are others, just as he said." She didn't want to ask if he was dead or not, but he must have understood something on her face. "He's alive. The injuries that he sustained are horrific, but he will survive if you can get him out now. You are still wanting to help me, right? Willing to go in and get him?"

"There is no question of me helping you. Just tell me what to do." He nodded and smiled. Dusty had no idea why he'd smile at a time like this, but he was moving down the hall and she had no choice but to follow. Dusty thought of Galin.

*Tell me where you are.* Dusty stopped walking for a second and looked around. She thought that Galin was standing right next to her when he spoke. *Where are you, love? Denise is beside herself with worry, Riss is spitting mad, and you don't even want to know what Kala and Judith are saying. I want to be with you.*

She told him what had happened. *You can't come. I'm not sure why I'm here either, but Jacob told me that I had to come. And if he had said you too, you'd be here with me. Boss isn't overly thrilled to have me here, I think.*

*Honey, Boss is here. With me and the others. He's not there. What's...do you know who might have you?* Dusty stilled in mid step. This was just wrong. *I will...please don't do anything. I don't know where you are but.... The only thing I can think of is that you're in another realm. Whoever this is, he's taken you to another realm for some reason. I'm betting it's Markum. There is no preparing for this. We can't get to you unless there is an invitation.*

*An invitation? Okay. Would you come and get my ass out of this mess?* He told her it didn't work that way. *Well, of course it doesn't. Why should it? I mean, I'm here and anyone who can save me is wherever you are. I want you to do me a favor. Don't tell Kip where I am.*

*He's not with you?* Her heart skipped several beats when Galin asked her. *The school said that you picked him up not an hour ago. I went there to get him knowing that he'd be worried if you weren't at home since you were working so hard. I assumed...Dusty, he must be there. That's why Jacob said you had to come with Boss.*

When whoever this man was turned to her, she had a feeling he knew just where Kip was. Before she could ask him, he pointed to a large cell door that looked like it was covered in blood, still dark and wet. She put out her hand to take the doorknob, then hesitated. There was just something not right about this whole thing. Turning to "Boss," she looked at him. Really looked, and realized what she should have at the very start. This was not the man she had been made to believe he was.

"You're not Him." Boss nodded and smiled at her. The smile was not reassuring, nor was it very friendly. "No, you're not. You look like Him, even sort of act like Him to a point, but you're so not Him."

"I'm your master. Believe me." She backed from the door. "Open it so that we may get out Jacob and the others. Kip needs you."

"Kip isn't in there." He nodded and she could see a part of this impostor that she'd not noticed before...he had dark wings. "You're not Boss, you're Markum."

The change was swift and scary. She watched in horrid fascination while the man she had come to admire more than anything disappeared and this...this monster took His place. When he moved toward her, she knew that she was seeing the real him and not the person he'd been when he'd come to her home and hurt Valyn.

He was taller by at least several feet. His wings were spread out now and she could see that not only were they dark, but they had hot veins of flames running through them. She took a step back when he sort of slithered toward her. His long torso was being held up by a serpent like body where legs should have been, and it had a long sharp point at the tail. And his entire body was encased in what looked like scales. He was fucking terrifying.

"You are much too smart for your own good. I've always thought that. Since I've found you, I kept thinking to myself, let her go, she'll get you into trouble. You have too, lots of it. But now you're here and you're mine." He spread his wings out more until they stretched the entire length of the area where they were. She could see that they were indeed dark...not black, but covered with blood. "You are going to be so much fun to fuck when this is finished. To think that I was going to give you to my lordship and not keep you for myself." He moved closer to her and she cringed from the stench.

"You will bow before me, Dusty McGee, and when you do, I shall take you and make you my pleasure bitch. And you'll only service me. Whenever and wherever I wish." He reached between his legs and stroked what she could only assume was a cock. He looked...she wanted to say tiny, but all she could think of was pencil dick.

"Are you kidding me? That's all you have? You're going to have to use a lot more than that if you want to fuck me. Can you...are you hard now? That doesn't even look like you could fuck an ant and have them feel it." His wrath burned over her skin when he roared at her. Dusty had no idea why pissing him off would make him be stupid, but the thought kept going around in her head like a loop. "I have an idea...why don't you go to my house and get a vibrator? I might come a couple of times if you use that; otherwise...otherwise, I'm not going to enjoy myself. And if I don't, you won't, buddy. I don't like to give when I get nothing in return. And with that...well, I'd get nothing for sure."

"You will be more respectful of me. I am going to be a lord and rule the realm with a hard fist." She giggled. "You think this is funny? You think that I'm not going to make you do as I say? I'm going to rule you. I'm going to make everyone bow before me, because I will be all powerful."

"All powerful with a tiny dick." His...claw, she supposed, came out and hit her before she could move. The pain was incredible but she didn't back down. He was mad now and backing himself into a corner, literally. As soon as she had him far from the doorway she'd come through she asked him about the door. "You had a real...well, I was going to say hard-on, but who knows with you. But you wanted me to open that door. Why? You brought me here thinking you were going to have an easy lay, and it all has to do with that door. What's on the other side, Markum of the Little Dick?"

"You'll not call me that again, woman. But you'll do as I command. You will see what I have for you. Open it." She looked at him like was he was not serious. "Come here then. Open it and we will enter together. Then I will show you what a real man can look like."

"I don't think so. You do it and maybe I'll go in with you." He roared again, and Dusty felt her skin blister. Much more of this and she'd be a crispy fry in no time. But he looked at the door. She could see the frustration on his face and the desperation. He wanted her in there and right now. Dusty wasn't going in there for all the money in the world.

"You will follow me?" She didn't say anything but shrugged. "I need for you to go willingly. If you do then I will return...he will be returned to you. I make this promise to you because you're going to do as I asked."

Dusty didn't point out that he hadn't asked anything but had kidnapped her, but kept her mouth shut. And by the person he said he was going to return to her, she didn't think he meant Kip because she knew that he was not in that room. There was something there, but it wasn't her Kip.

"What is the meaning of this?" They both turned to the second being that stood just inside the other hall, a hall she'd not noticed before now. "Who is this...this woman, and what is she doing here in this realm? What have you done, Markum?"

"She wanted to visit me and was thinking of staying, my lord. She has begged me so much that I thought it good that she come here." Dusty looked at Markum. There was such a marked change in him that she wanted to ask him who the being was. Markum's voice, his mannerisms, were all different. He was subservient sounding. Whoever this newcomer was, he was someone that Markum feared. But Dusty wasn't going to be a doormat any longer with this prick.

"He's lying to you. And big time too. He said he was keeping me for himself. And as far as visiting here? No way. I just came to find my nephew. I think this asshole took him from me and put him somewhere else. I don't know what's in that room, but he wants me to go in with him. I don't suppose you know what that's about, do you?" The being looked at her. "You should also know that I think he was going to fuck you over. And for some reason, I was the bait. Whatever his plans are, you are not going to come out on top as far as he's concerned."

The being—because she wasn't sure really what to call him—looked at the still closed door, then at Markum. She could see the anger there but also caution. When he spoke it was harsher than before, and a good deal angrier.

"You were taking her to your realm, your room?" Before Markum could say anything the being advanced to him. "You'll answer me truthfully or I will tear you apart. I've had enough of your shit to last several lifetimes. Answer me without a lie or so help me, I will give you such pain you will never recover from it."

"No, no, no. You can't believe her. She's just a woman. She lies. This woman begged me to make her my pleasure bitch. Mine. When I told her that you had to have her she told me that she'd rather die than to come to anyone but me." Markum looked at her. "She willingly came with me. Begged me to bring her here. I even asked her to stay behind because it was dangerous. Ask her, hear her lies as they spew from her mouth. I have never lied to you, my lord. She is the liar."

"Yeah, he did tell me that, but he wasn't him when he did it." She nodded when she realized how little sense she was making. "He looked like Boss. My friend. He even told me that he was coming here to save my friend and nephew. I'm pretty sure he's taken my protector and a few others too. I don't know why, but I think some of the protectors that are missing are in there. And I think he took them."

"You have a protector here?" There was no mistaking the anger now. The being practically boiled over with it. "You dare to bring a protector to this realm and hide them away and not tell me about it? What were you thinking? Or were you? Do you...have you...? Do you know what you have done? Do you know what will happen when He finds out what you have dared to do? I will not save you when He finds out. And He will. Even if I have to tell Him."

"I believe not only that he knows what he has done, but also had plans of continuing his scheme then laying the blame at your feet." Boss, the real one, bowed before her as He appeared and spoke. When he stood he winked at her before turning to the being. "You have taken what is mine without permission, Damon. I will want a full payment. There is no mistaking that this was a one-time event. He has at least nine of my men and women in there. And even though you claim not to be aware of it, they are still where they shouldn't be, and harmed too. What do you have to say about this?"

"He will pay." They all looked at Markum, who seemed to shrivel in size. Then Damon looked at her with a strange smile. "She called to you, didn't she? Called you to her, and now you have come."

"Nay. You know that she cannot. And you know what brought me here. It was not her saying my name." Damon nodded. "This is a grievous crime against my people, Damon. You and I both know that it is well within my rights to kill you both. But I will take payment due. You will pay me? And it will hurt him. Not just his body, because I'm sure you have plans for that, but with something he loves. If a man such as him can love."

"I believe you may be right in this. And I will make sure that he will pay you until he hurts. Then I will take my pounds of flesh." Dusty shivered, knowing that whatever was in store for Markum was not going to be something he walked away from any time soon. Damon bowed before smiling at her. "She is a great deal more than I would have thought on first look. You have done well this time."

"She is perfect."

# Chapter 9

They were all sitting around the table in her office. Kala and Riss were sitting in the chairs near her desk, as there was little room left elsewhere. Boss was not saying a word as all of them, and she did notice it was all of them, were shouting at him about one thing or another. Dusty simply watched. And thought.

"He will pay with his life; it is only fitting." Another said that Markum should be imprisoned for the rest of his days. Which she'd just found out was forever. Dusty did notice that Jacob said very little too. She supposed he was still trying to fight through the pain he was in. She looked up when someone sat on the floor near her.

"Are you all right?" She shrugged. Dusty didn't want to lie to Galin, but she wasn't really sure how to answer his question. "We can go home. There is no reason that you have to be here."

"I know. I just...I don't think I want to be alone right now." He nodded and took her hand. She knew that he'd be there with her, but Dusty needed the...well, the noise, she supposed. And something more to focus on than where she'd just been.

The man—it turned out he was called not just Damon, but Lord Damon—was in charge of most of the happenings in the other realm. The only person who had more authority was his boss, and no one wanted to bother him. Especially not Markum.

Lord Damon had sat down with her and Boss after Markum was…he disappeared, and that was all she knew for sure. She had an idea that he wasn't going to bother her or any of them ever again, but she didn't know precisely why. And she was pretty sure she never ever wanted to know why he wasn't there. Not having him there was enough for now.

"You will be given all that he has." Dusty didn't know what that meant and started to tell Damon no, she didn't want it, but Boss put his hand on her arm and she just nodded. "You'd do well to have Him guide you, my dear. You are a novice of the goings on here, and He will guide you well."

"He—Markum—said he had my nephew. Does he?" Damon closed his eyes then opened them.

"He did, but your nephew is now safe within your home." Dusty wanted to go to him now, but she'd been asked to come to this meeting of sorts and she knew that something important was going to be said and didn't want to miss it. "You have been harmed greatly by my minion. I am sorry for that. That is not the way we do business."

"Business?" Dusty waited for an explanation and when none was forthcoming, she asked what was forefront in her mind. "You said that I couldn't call out to Boss. And the two of you seemed to know why. Tell me. Please?"

Damon looked at Boss, who nodded slightly. When Damon stood up she thought he was going to show them out, as his face registered so much anger. When he handed her a small vial, she didn't take it until Boss told her it was all right.

"That is what true love looks like." She noticed that there was very little of anything at all in the vial and handed it back to him. "For my kind—and there are a great many of us—that is all we can expect to find here. But you...you were able to call to Boss because of your love for someone...I would say Galin...and in turn, this man."

"I don't understand. You said because I love Galin, I was able to call Boss to me? Why wouldn't I have called Galin?" Damon set the vial back on the pretty pedestal and sat back down. "You treasure that."

"I do. And in answer to your question, you have a great deal of love for this man too. Much more than would fit into this entire room and then some. Your love for your husband is infinity times that." Dusty nodded. She did love Galin, but she had never thought of it in volume before. "We do treasure it here. It is what...we must fight it daily to bring others to us."

"So love really is what makes the world go around." They both laughed but she stood up. Damon watched her carefully and she knew that if he tried anything, Boss would protect her. "What do you mean, I will get all that he has? Money?"

"Yes. And more. He will...Markum has been saving things for decades, and they too are worth a great deal of money." He put out his hand again and there was a large opal in it. "Not the most expensive gem in the world, by any means, but lovely. And he has a great deal of them. He collects them, you see."

"Money isn't the solve-all to this. He hurt my family. Markum burned a scar into my nephew, gave him horrific dreams." Damon nodded sadly as she continued. "Money will not make that all go away. It'll help him, but it won't negate the fact that he hurt him unnecessarily."

"It will not. But the mark has been removed. I cannot take the dreams away, but I can lessen them for him." Dusty shook her head. "You do not want me to take his dreams away?"

"I don't want you fucking with his mind. You just leave his mind to me." Damon nodded and smiled at her. "You will really leave him alone? No one here will ever bother him again?"

"You love him very much, do you not?" She nodded. "Then he will be safe from my kind for so long as he lives. And before you ask, that is a very long time. I have no designs over your nephew and none of my beings will ever reach out to him again."

"Thank you." Damon nodded and smiled again. "You do know that there is very little comfort in your smile. I don't mean to be mean but, damn, you're scary."

"I am supposed to be." She stepped back when he shifted. His body and face looked like every other person she knew. "This is much better for you?"

"It is, but not necessary. You should be your true self when you can. I don't want you to be someone you're not for me." He had nodded and went on to explain what she would need to do to claim the things that Markum was going to give her.

"Are you there?" Dusty looked up at Boss when He spoke. She'd been so deep in her thoughts that she'd not realized anyone had said her name. She looked around and saw that everyone was now gone.

"I guess I was thinking really hard." Boss smiled and sat down. "I still don't think we're safe, are we?"

"I would say for a time we are. But you will be all right, as well as Kipling." He handed her a box and she opened it. "Those are the most valuable gems that Markum had. I took the liberty of making sure the others are cashed out for you. The money is in a savings account with Kipling's name on it. Yours as well, but I believe you will want him to have it."

"He wants to go to college. It will help." Boss smiled and nodded. Dusty ran her fingers over the diamonds and emeralds, along with a few other pieces she had no name for. "And these? What do you want me to do with these?"

"I would suggest you buy this building from Judith. Then sell your small home and purchase something bigger for your family. Galin has monies too. A great deal of it that, I'm sure, you will put to good use over the years." He laughed a little and she looked at Him. "The fund for Kipling will be enough for him to go to any college he wants and never worry about working. He is very set."

"I'm glad." She was too. Kipling wanted to be a lawyer and she was sure that didn't come with a small price tag. "I can't have children."

"Nay, you cannot. But you can have them if you want them." She looked up at Him, confused. "Adopt them with Galin. You will have no problems doing so. Judith and Agon will be able to advise you on this, as they are doing it now."

"She told me." Still she fingered the gems. "I want to be helpful, but I just don't know why you picked me. If you need someone to advertise an event or a product, even make up some business cards, I'm on it, but there is very little else I can do with your Mystics."

"Why do you think that?" She snorted at him and He laughed. "I see that you have put a great deal of thought into this. So I will be straight forward with you. I do not need advertising. It's not something that we do. Nor do I need business cards. I have no phone and no email address, so there would be nothing on it save my name. And Boss would not be something I'd like for people to see on a card. I think it would turn them off. As for what you can do…well, there are a great many things. But…."

"You're not going to tell me." He shook His head. "You do know that I can be much better at helping if You simply told me what it is You want me to do."

"But that would be no fun for me." He stood up and kissed her forehead. "Love Galin. He needs that from you, and in turn, I do as well. And go home. Kipling has invited me to dinner, and I am looking forward to sesame chicken with brown rice."

~~~

Galin helped Kip clean up the kitchen. They'd sent Dusty for some ice cream when they decided that they wanted a snack after Boss had left. She had left them to clean up the kitchen and Galin was enjoying the job. Except that he'd already broken a cup and a plate in his job of drying them.

"You keep it up and we'll need a whole new kitchen." Galin looked at the tea maker he'd killed earlier. "You promise to read the instructions from now on, right?"

"You said to pour the water into the container and turn it on. I didn't know you meant to put the water in the back of the thing." He grinned. "I'm really glad you had a fire extinguisher. Who knew that flames could get that high?"

"I did." Kip handed him a large bowl and told him to be careful with it. He washed two more pieces before he continued talking. "I guess you and Aunt Dusty will want to have your own family now."

"We have one." Galin put the bowl on the table, thrilled he'd not even chipped it. "You're our family now. I'm your uncle and Dusty will still be your aunt."

"I mean kids of your own." Galin started to laugh but realized that the boy was hurting. "Aunt Dusty said something a while back about sending me to a boarding school."

"Do you want to go there?" Kip shook his head. "Then why would we push you away when we have only just gotten to know you? As for children, we cannot have any of our own. I'm not human."

"But Aunt Dusty is." Galin shook his head. "So she's like you? Someone who will live forever and ever. But not me."

"Not yet." Kip stopped washing the pan that was in his hand and stared at him. "I can prolong your life if you wish. I can't do it now as you are but a child, but when you are older, I can if you still wish it."

"You mean if you did it now, I'd still be a kid in about fifty years." Galin nodded. "Thanks for not doing it then. Being a kid sucks."

They both laughed and before they were finished, Galin broke the big bowl. He'd been very careful when putting it into the cabinet, but he'd set another bowl above it and it fell out of his hand and hit it. Galin wanted to cry. He'd never been this clumsy before.

"We need a dishwasher." Galin agreed with Kip as they cleaned up the mess. "I'm not sure, but I think we'd be better off with a lot of things you can't break. You're sort of dangerous."

"I'm unused to doing domestic chores. I want to learn them, but there are so many things…the microwave boggles my mind in what can and can't go in it. The refrigerator with the ice machine still confuses me. Where does the water come from if not from someplace magical?" Galin knew it was from a small hose, as Kip had pulled out the refrigerator and showed him, but still…. "And the television. How is it that you have over a thousand stations, yet you complain about nothing being on? I have seen plenty on. You just…you zoom past the shows as if you're in a race to see how many you can pass in a minute."

"I've seen it all." Kip put the towel he'd been using to wipe down the counter on the back of the chair. "I have another question for you. You can say no if you want, but I'd really like you to think about it. I've already asked Aunt Dusty and she's thinking on it too, though she wanted to answer me right then, but…can I call you Dad instead of Uncle Galin?"

Galin staggered back from the boy. To be called Dad was something he'd never thought to be called. He sat down and stood up twice before he pulled Kip into his arms and hugged him to him. He had a son.

"Is that a yes?" Galin laughed. "Aunt Dusty did the same thing. Not the hopping up and down thing, but she hugged me tight enough to cut off my air."

Galin let him go immediately but pulled him back for another, quicker hug. "You have given me a great gift. One that I never thought to own. I don't…words fail me in this. I have…you…I would be truly honored if you were to call me Dad. And more so to call you son."

"Yeah, Aunt…Mom said that I'd given her more than she could ever tell me. I guess…you guys drive me nuts sometimes, but I think I love you." Kip laughed. "Okay, I really love you. And I've never had a dad before so…we'll have to figure this out together."

"I would be glad to have you as a teacher." Kip nodded and said he had homework. Galin sat at the table to wait for Dusty. He had a son. Galin was still smiling about it when Dusty walked in the door fifteen minutes later.

"He asked you." Galin nodded and pulled her into his lap. "He had me bawling like a little baby when he asked me. He told me that his mom was always Rose to him since she never wanted anyone to know she had a son his age. But he said I'm his mom now and forever."

"We will give him a good life." Dusty nodded and leaned her head on his shoulder. "I should like to ask you something as well. I have…there is a house that I would like for us to purchase. It is in a safer neighborhood and closer to Kip's school. As well as your business."

"Judith called me on the way back from the store." Dusty got up and started pulling down bowls. When she noticed the large empty place where her bowl had been, he got up to get spoons. "You're no longer allow in the kitchen. Anyway, she wants me to buy Strategize from her, the building. She said she'd give me a good deal."

"Will you do it?" She nodded and Galin smiled. "Then we should celebrate somehow. I have a job as well. I'm going to be working with the Mystic's and Riss. They've asked me to train the others on how to find minions when they are at a home. I can see them and thought that all of us could."

As they ate their ice cream with Kip, Galin brought up the house again. "It's near the downtown area and is close to the library. I have…to be honest, I already bought it. Long ago, but we own it. It's the house that sits next to the bank."

"The big blue one?" Galin nodded and watched as both Kip and Dusty stared at each other before she looked at him again. "The big blue one with the fenced in back yard, the pool, and the five bedrooms?"

"Yes. Though the pool is empty now there's nothing wrong with it." He frowned at them. "How do you know so much about this house already?"

"I have wanted that house since…well, it seems like forever. And the other day, Kip and I walked around to the backyard and talked about how cool it would be to own it. And now we do." She squealed and got up to dance around the room. Kip and he just watched her. She finally sat down and laughed again.

"I don't think I've ever seen you this excited before. Would you like to go and see it tomorrow?" They both nodded. "Okay. We'll make it a date. Then we'll go and make an offer on Strategize."

An hour later, after he'd managed to break another bowl when cleaning up, he followed Dusty to their bedroom. She'd been so excited all evening, and he wanted to simply hold her and absorb some of her excitement. When they got to the room, she sat on the bed and looked at him.

"I've been thinking of you all day." He nodded and leaned against the dresser and watched her. "About you making love to me. About the things I want to do to you."

"What are they?" She laid back and he moved toward her. His cock ached and he wanted to show her how much she meant to him. But the second he was close to the bed, she sat up and rubbed her cheek over his shaft.

"I want to take you into my mouth and have you come down my throat." He nodded and helped her open his pants. Before he was completely free of them, she licked his crown and had him moan. "You're so hard and thick. I love the feeling of you inside of me. Taking me hard."

"I need you." She shook her head and pulled his pants to his thighs. When she took him into her mouth, Galin curled his fingers into her hair. He had thought to hold on but he found himself pumping her as if it were her womanhood. "I will come this way."

She looked up at him, never taking her mouth from him. When she cupped his bottom, pulling him closer, Galin wanted to come right then, but she pulled back and looked at him.

"Will you come on me? I want to feel your hot cum on my body." She ran her hands down her ribs to her legs and was gloriously naked. "I need this."

He never got the chance to answer her because she took him again. This time she worked hard at having him release sooner than he really wanted. Her warm fingers cupped his balls, and when she rolled them in her fingers, he could no longer hold back. Pulling free of her mouth, Galin fisted his cock as he released. When some of his seed touched her mouth, she licked it in and then rubbed the rest over her body. Dropping to his knees, Galin pulled her legs apart and took her small nubbin into his mouth and nipped hard.

Her scream was cut off and he looked up at her. She was screaming into a pillow and he smiled. Leaning back to her dewy curls, Galin feasted on her until she released several more times and begged him to stop. Lifting his head when she pulled him up by his hair, he thought she was the most beautiful creature ever made.

"Take me." Crawling up her body, he took her nipple into his mouth as he slid into her. She was so wet that he moved in and out of her without any resistance. As soon as her legs wrapped around his hips, Galin started to move in and out of her slowly. Even when she begged him to take her harder, he slowed even more.

"I love seeing you this way, your need all over your body. Your nipples hard and pink from my mouth." He rolled his hips and she moaned loudly. "When you release I will fill your body with my seed and bring you to peak again."

"Please." He kissed her throat, and then took her earlobe into his mouth and bit down on it as well. When she cried out, her body bowing up off the bed when she released, Galin threw back his head and emptied himself inside of her. Then she tightened around him again, Galin pinched her tight nipple between his thumb and finger and held her while she released again and again. Dropping down on top of her, he rolled to his back, taking her with him.

"When we move into the house, I'd like to have our bedroom as far from Kips as we can get. That way I can scream my head off when you make me come like that." He laughed and pulled her tighter to him. "And maybe we can look into getting some toys to use too. It might be a lot of fun."

Galin had already been looking and had a list now. Before he could tell her what he had in mind, he noticed that she'd fallen asleep in his arms. Galin held her all night and let her sleep in while he and Kip made breakfast. And for once, he didn't break a single thing.

# Chapter 10

"The list of your punishments is there for you to read." Markum didn't bother looking at them. They'd been told to him several times now. "You will read them and tell me that you agree with them."

"Agree with them? Are you…? No, I don't agree with them. I was simply trying to bring someone to our realm that would be fun. Damon said it would be wonderful. He and Anthony, it was their idea." Markum had been blaming them both since he'd been taken from right outside his room the other day. And now this. "You should really see what your management is up to. I'm pretty sure you would find out all kinds of things."

"I have." Markum looked at his lordship, Oscar he'd heard the other man call him, and swallowed hard. That didn't sound good. "As of yesterday, I have taken it upon myself to look into what else you might have been doing. And you'd be surprised at how much I've found —"

"They lie." He flushed when the being cocked a brow at him. "They all are lying about everything. I'm not nearly as bad as they're painting me to be."

"And how badly do you suppose they've painted you? I have a very extensive list here. Would you like to hear what some of them are?" Markum shook his head. "Too bad. The first thing I found out, quite by accident, was that you have been to the other realm at least daily. You are not set to go there as a minion, much less as a demi-god."

"I didn't go daily." He hadn't. He would skip a day now and then so that he could rest up and dream. Some of the things they had in the other realm were just too wonderful to not want. "Whoever told you that was not telling the truth."

"Do you ever suppose there will be a time when something I say about you isn't a lie?" Markum considered answering that but was cut off before he could think of a good lie. Just about everything he said was a lie of some form or another, and it was hard for him to separate fact from fiction at times. Like he ever bothered, he thought with a laugh. "When in the other realm it was discovered that you have become a thief. Not a bad trait among humans, but you are not one. When you steal there, it reflects badly on us."

"How so? I mean, we're considered bad anyway. What does the fact that I might steal a few things when I go to visit matter?" Markum thought about what he'd said. "If I went to visit. I'm not saying I have but if I did, why shouldn't I be able to bring back a souvenir once in a while?"

Another minion walked into the room and handed a large box to his lordship. When it was dumped on the table, Markum smiled at what lay there. His things. Pretty things he just couldn't live without. He reached for one of them and his hand was slapped away. The burning had him putting his hand into his mouth.

"This is from one day. I know this because you were stupid enough to mark the dates on the box when you stored them in your realm." The box was turned and there it was, the date. Eight days ago, as a matter of fact. "Just how stupid are you?"

Markum didn't answer. He wasn't sure it was a real question so he kept nursing his hand. When the next box was brought in and dumped on the table, Markum knew better than to reach for anything. When Oscar picked up something Markum had yet to figure out, he wanted to snatch it from him. Instead he just glared.

"I have nothing to say about these things. I can only think that someone wanted to frame me and put these things into my realm. You might want to add that to your list of things to look into." Oscar sat down but held the same device in his hand. "That does not belong to you. You should put it back and then have someone take it back to my room. I'll take care of it getting back to the owner." Namely him.

"You just don't get it, do you?" Markum shook his head. If he understood what was going on, he knew he'd be better prepared to deal with this. "You are not going back to your room, you're not going to get your things, and as far as I can see, you will more than likely be gone before this meeting has ended. I'm astounded by you."

"Thank you." He'd never astounded anyone before. "But I don't think it will do any of us any good if you put me into prison. There are any number of people who have done far worse than me. Like you for instance. I think you've been guilty of stealing a few things here and there. What about my rocks? You took them, didn't you?"

"I gave them to the woman. Along with your other stones." Markum stood up and started to go and get them back when he felt himself slammed against the wall. "Sit down."

"I will have my things. I have taken a great deal of time and effort in getting them, and I want them back." He slammed his hand down on the table to show how serious he was. It didn't have the same effect that he'd hoped for. Oscar laughed and laughed hard. When he stopped laughing, just having an occasional little one, he looked at him.

"You are hereby sentenced to death. There will be a beating first with your skin flayed from your back, then you will have your nails taken from your hands one at a time and acid put upon the open wounds to burn for the rest of your day. And when you have suffered greatly with this you will—"

Markum had had enough. "I want you to stop this right now. You're not going to kill me. I forbid it." Oscar laughed again and Markum nodded. "There you see, it was a joke. You will not kill the best demi-god you've ever had simply because he was caught. What kind of place are you running here when a man can't have some fun?"

The pain started in his belly. Looking down he realized that while he wasn't hurt, he felt as if he was on fire. Putting his hand on his skin, it felt hot. Like nearly three hundred degrees hot. And he knew his heat. Standing up, he looked at Oscar as he stood as well. The smile on his face terrified him.

"What have you done?" Oscar didn't answer but left him in the room. The longer he stood there the hotter he got. Moving his hand over his belly again he knew that if this didn't stop soon he was going to be dead. Surely someone would come and take this away soon. Going to the door, he pounded on it.

"This is enough now, you've made your point. Come back here now, please. I'll behave." He pounded harder when he felt his skin begin to peel away from the bone. "You'll need to hurry. I don't think I have much time left."

As his belly spilled onto his feet, Markum backed up and sat on the table. His things were still there and he picked one of them up and held it to his cheek. If someone was going to save him, they'd get all of his things. He'd gladly give them to whoever came into this room.

Weak now, he lay on the table. The pain was incredible. As each of his limbs began to fall off him, he mourned their loss. Markum was afraid now that no one was coming back. And just as he was ready to give up, he saw Oscar.

"Thank you. I thought you'd been teaching me a lesson and it went too far." The man snapped his fingers and Markum screamed. Screamed until there was nothing left of his face and throat to do so. Just as he was fading out, Oscar came into his view.

"You shall endure this daily for the rest of my days. You will wake being whole, and by days end you will be suffering this ten times ten. Good bye, Markum." Then he was no more.

~~~

They were moving into the house when his phone rang. It was still something he had to get used to, and if Kip hadn't told him, again, that his butt was ringing, he might not have answered it. But when he saw Dusty's face come up on the screen he simply smiled.

"If you answer it you can hear her voice too." Kip laughed as he walked away. It took him two tries but he finally got the call answered.

"Having trouble again?" She laughed and Galin smiled. He would gladly mess up all the time to hear her do that again. "I have some news. I was able to get a good price on the building."

She'd been trying for days to get Judith to sell her the building. It wasn't as if she didn't want to sell it to them, but she didn't want a good asking price. Galin was still trying to familiarize himself with the currency here, but even he thought that five bucks wasn't very much.

"What sort of price are you going to pay her?" She told him. "And that is enough for you to be happy with? I should think that you'd need to pay more."

"Remind me not to take you on negotiations with me. And yes, that's a good price. As of tomorrow morning, we'll own it as well. Are you ready to celebrate again?" He was nodding before she finished. "I was thinking we could go to that new restaurant in town."

His disappointment was profound. The last time they had celebrated he could barely walk for a whole day. They'd just tried out a new piece of equipment they'd purchased for their new bedroom, and Dusty had proved that she loved being the one in charge as much as he did. They were now going to take turns.

"I was thinking after dinner we could come to our new home and break in the bed. Not break it, but break it in." He flushed. "I promise not to break this one. It was very embarrassing when I had to explain to the man why we needed a new bed."

"You didn't have to tell him anything. It's not required for you to explain everything to everyone, you know?" He'd been told that before. Like when they'd ordered a new set of dishes, which he promptly dropped and broke every one of them. He'd told the sales person that he was accidently breaking things all the time and that he thought it was because he wasn't used to being in this realm. She had hurried away so quickly that he'd not been able to ask her about a different color on the dishes.

But Dusty told him it would be great...just not to touch her tea cup collection. He glanced over at the box that he'd nearly dropped and would have if not for Kip. He owed the boy a great deal. As soon as he hung up he told Kip what they were doing for dinner.

"That's cool. But if you don't mind, I'd like to stay here and set up my new room. The bed will be here in an hour and I'm really psyched to get it going." Galin said that would be fine and helped him bring in the rest of the boxes. All but the ones marked with Kip's name. They'd been marked that way so he'd know not to touch them. And after helping pack some of the things he avoided those boxes as much as he could.

Riss showed up about the time Kip's bedroom set did, and they all worked to put it together. Dan was called in as neither Galin nor Riss had any clue how to read, much less follow instructions, and the room was finished in no time. Dan even hung around to help hang a few shelves that Dusty had wanted. All in all it was a good day.

He and Riss moved out to the back deck when Dan left. "I'm to tell you that the money is in your account." Galin nodded, relieved. He had been waiting on some word of it for a few days. He had no idea what the amount was, but was assured it was enough. "The banker said to tell you that you'd have to invest some of it. They have limits on how much they can hold in one place."

"I'll do that in the morning." They sat on the new chairs and looked out over the pool. "You're here for something more. What is it?"

"I should like your help. I have...I have a young woman who works for me that is very standoffish. I believe she has been hurt, but I cannot get anyone to tell me what has brought her to us. She is solely human."

"Did you check with Boss?" Riss nodded. "Let me guess; he told you all in good time. It seems to be a favorite line of his."

"Actually, he said that he will tell me on the morrow. I think that was three days ago. I think...I believe the girl is lost."

A lost soul. That was bad. But what was she doing with a bunch of protectors and Mystic's then? Before he could ask any more questions, Michael appeared. He looked like he'd been in a fight.

"I am trying to learn how to use that trampoline that is at the compound." Riss looked shocked but Galin started laughing. "I have discovered that not only is it impossible to walk on it, but it is most difficult to get off as well. I had to call for assistance with it."

"What were you wearing when you were on it?" Michael looked down at his clothing and Galin laughed harder. "You do know that it's probably not all that smart to carry a sword on one of those things. You could cut your leg off."

In answer, Michael pulled up his kilt and showed them the long gash from his thigh to his knee. Galin laughed so hard that he was sure he'd broken a rib or two. He was still laughing when Dusty got home. And telling her about it nearly made him have to lie down. Galin had never laughed this hard in his life. Life was very good right now. And Galin was looking forward to many more days like the one he'd had today.

# About the Author

Kathi Barton, author of the bestselling series Force of Nature, lives in Nashport, Ohio with her husband Paul. In addition to writing full time Kathi likes to spend time with her eight grandkids, three children and three children-in-laws. She writes to relax and have fun.

Her muse, a cross between Jimmy Stewart and Hugh Jackman brings them to life for her readers in a way that has them coming back time and again for more. Her favorite genre is paranormal romance with a great deal of spice. You can visit Kathi on line and drop her an email if you'd like. She loves hearing from her fans. aaronskiss@gmail.com.

Follow Kathi on her blog:
http://kathisbartonauthor.blogspot.com/

www.ingramcontent.com/pod-product-compliance
Lightning Source LLC
Chambersburg PA
CBHW032129170626
46808CB00006B/2154